TAME ME

THE MACINTYRE BROTHERS: BOOK THREE

S. E. LUND

TAME ME
THE MACINTYRE BROTHERS SERIES: BOOK THREE

 Created with Vellum

1

ELLA

I ALWAYS LOVED CHRISTMAS IN NEW HAMPSHIRE.

Over the years, our family had spent time in tropical locations during the Christmas and New Year's holidays, but I always loved when we stayed in town. I loved the snow at that time of year. It felt more like real Christmas, especially with the lights decorating the streets and the big Christmas tree in the city plaza. The annual Christmas parade was something I always looked forward to as a child.

So, I usually anticipated Christmas with a great deal of excitement.

Unfortunately, this year, I dreaded it because I knew that my father, The Governor, would be grilling Josh like he was a prime catch of the day.

Which, of course, he was.

My mother was in seventh heaven at the thought I was engaged to one of the wealthiest bachelors in all of America. She actually held her hand over her heart when I told her about our engagement after our weekend at Josh's beach house in Montauk.

"Oh, my *God*, I think I'll faint," she said when we Skyped the following Tuesday after I got back into town. I could see tears forming in her eyes. "You're engaged? To Josh? My goodness, that was fast. And here I thought that you two were going to break up!"

"I know," I said. "I thought we were going to as well, but I was wrong. When Josh explained what happened with Penny, I had to kick myself for being so quick to think he'd cheated on me."

"Old wounds leave a scar," she said, wiping her eyes and smiling. "Sometimes, it makes it harder to trust, but it often makes us that much stronger. What doesn't kill you, right?"

With Christmas was just a few days away, it was time for Josh to meet my father and hopefully, quell all the questions he had about Josh's dad.

I hoped so. I didn't want any hard feelings between them, especially over the holidays. We had ten days off -- ten glorious days -- and I wanted them to count. We were going to spend a few with the parental units before flying to California so I could finally meet David. Josh's brother insisted that we come out for a few days and stay with him at the mansion, and Josh had asked me if I'd be willing.

"Of course," I said and smiled enthusiastically when Josh asked. "I'd love to meet your family. All your brothers."

"They're going to LA to stay with David, so it will be a real family get together. I don't want to miss it and I want to be with you. I'm greedy that way."

"I'm all yours," I said. "We'll spend two days with my mom and dad, and then we'll go to LA. You're the boss."

He tickled me. "Don't say that," he said. "Makes me feel guilty, like I'm taking advantage of my power over you as your employer."

"You're not paying me, so I don't think it matters."

"Oh, so that's the solution, is it? Hire beautiful women and seduce them but make sure not to pay them? Is that how it works?"

He pulled me into his arms, and we kissed. I loved it when we teased each other. He laughed so easily and was a bit of a rascal.

He was fun to be with.

Jerkface had been so serious, so focused on his career, and moving up the corporate ladder that I always felt like an interloper in his life. Like he'd made this small space for me to fit into and made sure I didn't impinge on the rest of his carefully arranged life.

Josh was the opposite. He was very busy, of course, as the CEO of MBC, and all its subsidiaries, and of course, his hands-on management of the *Chronicle*, but I felt totally integrated in his life. A priority.

That meant a lot to me. I wasn't just an add-on, and I wasn't a means to a business end, the way I had been with Jerkface.

So, I approached the holidays with a mix of happiness and trepidation. How would my father treat him?

"Mom, you have to tell Dad not to interrogate Josh about the business back with Mr. Garner," I said when we were on the phone talking about our plans. "Josh had nothing to do with it."

"I know, dear," my mother said. "I'll give him the word."

I could almost see her pointing her finger at my father and telling him to be nice and respectful to Josh and not to pester him about Josh Sr's history with his former business partner. She was no shrinking violet.

"My Josh had nothing to do with all that intrigue and scandal," I added. "It was long before he was even out of high school so if there's any guilt, it's not on my Josh's shoulders."

"He knows that, dear, but it's hard for him to forget what happened. Don't worry. He'll be on his best behavior. I promise I'll have him whipped into shape by Christmas."

She laughed and I had to smile, although I wasn't entirely sure she was right. He had a mind of his own and was a man of power. He was used to getting what he wanted, and I knew he'd never felt as if Josh's father paid any price for what happened.

Frankly, I didn't really know what happened, except that the nightly investigative news show that was the pride of Macintyre Broadcasting Corporation did a hard-hitting exposé of Mr. Garner that led to a criminal investigation and in the end, his incarceration for fraud. If he hadn't been guilty, I felt certain that the courts would have let him go. The fact that he went to jail satisfied me that whatever role MBC had in the affair, the sentence was warranted.

Anyway, Josh was in school when it all happened so there was no way he had anything to do with it. My father would just have to forget it and move on.

On his part, Josh spent the night before we went to Concord on his computer, while I spent it watching *Oliver!*, a movie he said he and his brothers and father always watched at Christmas and eating popcorn.

"Josh," I called out from the living room of his apartment. "Come and watch. I thought you said you watch this every Christmas."

"I do, I do," he replied. "I just have a bit of work to finish up before I can feel comfortable taking the rest of the holiday off and join you. Go ahead and watch without me."

I shrugged, and pressed play on the remote, wanting to watch with him, but I had to realize he had a very responsible position with MBC and the *Chronicle*. I couldn't begrudge him trying to finish up work before taking a vacation.

I watched for an hour before I got up for a pee break and passed the office. Josh was bent over his laptop, reading some kind of document online. When I was finished, I stopped in and leaned over him, kissing his neck.

"What are you working so hard on?" I asked. I checked his computer screen and saw an old news clipping that looked like it was on microfiche.

VP of Centaur Corp Indicted on 15 Charges of Insider Trading, Going to Jail

I squeezed his shoulder. "Josh," I said and leaned my chin on his shoulder. "You said you had work to do. This isn't work."

He turned around and pulled me onto his lap. I giggled when he tickled me, squirming out of the way, but he was stronger, and I couldn't escape.

"*Au contraire, ma petit*, this is real work. This is understanding the case well enough that I can face your father and answer all his questions about it when I meet him this weekend."

"I don't want you two talking about the case," I said. "I want peace between you. It's off limits, okay?"

"You know he'll say something about it," Josh said. "I have to be able to answer."

"Seriously, no," I replied and pushed his shoulder. "Be a good boy, okay? My mom will work on my dad to keep his mouth shut, too. We want a peaceful happy Christmas."

On his part, Josh kissed me to silence my protest and I was momentarily lost in his arms and to his very passionate kiss. I knew it was just a ruse to distract me from what he was doing.

I pulled away and squeezed his shoulder. "Don't try to use your sexy body to distract me," I said and narrowed my eyes. "If you think you can manipulate me with your hunky muscles and passion, you're wrong."

"Ha!" he said and squeezed me. "It worked last night when you asked me about it. It worked again this morning when you tried again. I figured it would work again tonight."

"You think I'm that easy, do you?" I asked, mock-upset.

"I count on it," he replied and smiled at me in this totally seductive way. I couldn't help but smile back.

"I have this weakness for you," I said. "Don't condemn me."

"I know, and I intend to exploit that weakness as often as I can."

We kissed again and then his cell dinged, interrupting us.

He glanced over at his cell. "I have to answer this," he said and picked it up, reading the message. "It's from my legal team. They're sending me some files on the case, so I understand all the ins and outs."

"Josh, you shouldn't feel like you're going to an interrogation. It's Christmas. We're going to go spend two days with my parents, open presents, have Christmas dinner and try to have a nice time. My mother's been working on my father to keep his questions to himself -- at least for the holidays. I'm sure you two will talk about it at some point, just to clear the air, but please. Not at Christmas..."

"I don't want to talk about it, but I know it will be on your father's mind and I want to be ready. It's my business now. I want to know what happened. Your father deserves a straight answer and some evidence to back it all up."

"Bah, Humbug," I said and pouted. "If you two do talk about it, I don't want it to ruin the time we have together."

"It won't," he said and squeezed me again. "I promise."

I stared into his blue eyes, taking in a deep breath, and deciding that I could trust him to finesse things with my father if the issue came up.

"Will you come and watch the rest of the movie with me?" I asked, giving him my best pout. "You said it was your favorite..."

"I will as soon as I read over the messages and reply. Okay?"

"Okay," I said, and we kissed again. Finally, I left him to his cell phone and messages with his legal team and went back to the living room and Oliver!

I grabbed my bag of microwave popcorn and snuggled into the sofa, pressing play on the movie, and waited for him to come and join me. My father's history with Josh's father was the only issue between us that caused me any concern. We had cleared the air about Penny's treatment and the need for Josh to keep in touch with the facility and with Penny, but he included me in on that whenever he got an email or phone call about her progress. She had a few weeks left on her treatment schedule and would be getting released in the new year. I hoped that would be the end of it and she'd be sober and could move on with her life. I hoped that Josh's involvement in her life would end at that point, but I had a feeling that no matter what, he would be responsible for her in some way.

She sounded like a very needy person to me. Someone who saw Josh as a cash cow that she could milk for more money when she needed it. It was sad but true that people with a lot of wealth often had to suspect other people's motives. They never knew whether the friendship or romance was due to the money or to themselves as a person.

At least with Josh and I, he knew from the start that I liked him before I knew he was one of the wealthiest men in America. I liked him before I knew he was my boss. He liked me because I didn't know who he was because he could trust that I liked him for him. Not his money. He liked me despite not needing my father's power and influence to get him anywhere. Josh was his own man and didn't need anyone else's help to succeed.

Sure, he had all the benefits of an upper-class upbringing, but from what I had read and what Josh told me, the boys were expected to work and support themselves, although they always had access to their trust funds for investment purposes. Their father had supported them in their various ventures, but he had expected them to put in public service in the military or national guard in return. It made me respect him even more, if possible. Any of us with Joshua Sr's money would have done the same and provided the best upbringing possible. At least their father had tried to impart a work ethic in his sons, and they weren't spoiled brats, living the high life without responsibilities.

I knew that when the time came, Josh would be an excellent father. He'd had a wonderful role model. I could tell that by how decent and hard working all the sons were -- even David, the rocker, was a self-made man, starting out in garage bands in high school and working the bar circuits with his band before they hit it big. He didn't buy his way onto the radio waves.

I checked my watch. Another hour had passed, and Josh was still in his office, poring over the documents his lawyers had sent.

"Josh Macintyre Jr," I called out. "Get in here, now, or you'll have a very unhappy girlfriend..."

I turned back to the television and before I could pick up the bag of popcorn, Josh vaulted over the back of the sofa and plopped down beside me. He stretched out his legs onto the coffee table and grabbed the bag of popcorn.

"You mean fiancée. I thought I'd upgraded you from girl-friend to soon-to-be-new-bride."

"Your soon-to-be-new-bride wants you at her side."

"I'm all yours," he said and stuffed a handful of kernels into his mouth, which was currently grinning.

I smiled and reached for the bag.

"What are we watching again?" he asked, a playful expression in his eyes. "Something about Oliver Cromwell?"

I pushed him with my shoulder. "Be quiet and hand over the bag."

For the next two hours, we watched the movie and spent our first Christmas together following one of his family traditions.

I felt so happy saying that -- his family traditions that I was now a part of.

It felt good.

2

JOSH

I thought my research would just help me understand what happened so many years earlier with my father and Ella's father. What it did was alarm me, for it seemed that Henry Garner wasn t the only one involved in the insider trading.

Ella's father had been as well.

How he escaped getting caught up in the scandal, I didn't know.

Frankly, I wasn't sure I really wanted to know.

What happened was old news. Garner did his time in a cushy prison for white collar criminals, and then lawyer Emmet Carlson went on to do very well in state politics.

Finished. End of story.

Except... not.

There was some reason Emmet himself wasn't charged. There was no record of him being charged and pleading down in exchange for his testimony against Garner. He just was never even a target of the investigation. That didn't make sense to me. He was the man's business partner. They'd invested together but for some reason, only the partner was charged.

I wracked my brain trying to figure out why Carlson escaped justice, but Garner didn't.

What I came up with was nothing. Zip. He was just never a suspect or charged with any crime in connection to Garner's financial wrangling so he either was innocent, or there was another reason he got off scot-free.

I should have just let it go at that. Justice was served. The state had its chance to charge Emmet Carlson and had not chosen to do so.

That was it.

But it nagged at my brain...

I sat staring at the computer screen and then typed a response in to Ted, one of the lawyers who worked for MBC.

JOSH: *Why did he get off when Garner didn't? Any thoughts?*

TED: *Your guess is as good as mine. The insider trading had to do with stocks from a foreign corporation. Either Carlson had a friend in the justice department, or he was somehow working at a higher level and got immunity in return for his evidence. It's unclear how Garner got caught. Who can say?*

JOSH: I don't suppose I can just ask Governor Carlson why. Wouldn't that be a great topic of dinner conversation the first weekend I meet my soon-to-be in-laws...

TED: I wouldn't recommend it. Something was up with this case. Either Carlson is a mole working for the Fed's FinCEN network, or the system itself is corrupt and he paid someone off and Garner took the fall. I can ask around and see what turns up if you'd like.

JOSH: Hold off on that for a while. I'm not sure I want to turn over this stone at this time.

ED: You're the boss. I can make very discreet enquiries in case you're worried.

JOSH: How about we put this on hold until after the holidays and revisit in the new year?

ED: Sounds good. Let me know.

JOSH: I will. Thanks for your discretion and have a great holiday.

ED: You as well.

I exhaled and rubbed my eyes, feeling like I'd stumbled into something I probably should have just ignored for my own personal good, but I couldn't. I worked in military intelligence when I was in the service and my mind worked in a way that I couldn't just shut down at will. My biggest concern was how I would broach the issue with Ella. I didn't want to say anything to her about my suspicions before I knew more because it would really upset her for no reason if there was no 'there' there. If there was any substance to my doubts about the case, I would tell her the truth. Until then, discretion was the better part of valor, or so they say. I had to hope that I would find nothing out about Emmet Carlson that might make me regret looking in the first place.

I had only wanted to be able to explain things to him about MBC's coverage of the scandal. I hadn't wanted to open up a whole new can of worms...

Ella called from the living room and I knew I had to shut down my mind for the rest of the evening and spend it with my bride-to-be. She deserved my complete attention when I was with her, so I closed the documents I'd been reading, shut off my email and Skype window, and I took in a deep breath. I'd blank the whole matter from my mind and focus on the movie. It was a perennial favorite of my brothers and of course, one of my own favorite movies and Christmas traditions.

It felt good to be including Ella in that tradition. I hoped we would make new traditions of our own that we could pass down to our children and them to theirs.

Smiling to myself as I thought about it, I went to the living room, hopped over the back of the sofa and landed beside Ella. I grabbed the popcorn and started to eat, pretending like all was right with the world. She would only find out about my suspicions when there was some substance behind them and not until.

I loved her too much to worry her needlessly.

I'd been wrong before about these matters, but I had a pretty good instinct for suspicious behavior.

I hoped I was wrong this time.

W e drove to Concord on Christmas Eve, and arrived just before supper. The sky was overcast, and the lights in the city gave it a festive feeling.

"What's the protocol for the night? Will we be sleeping together? Will I be in the doghouse in the backyard?"

Ella reached over and took my hand. "I already spoke with Mom. She said she fixed up the spare room for you."

I laughed. "I guess that settles it."

"Yeah, she wouldn't mind personally, but it's my dad. He's a bit old fashioned in that way."

"What about when you move in with me? What will he do after that?"

"What do you mean, when I move in with you? You mean after we get married?"

I kissed her knuckles. "No. Before. I want us to find an apartment together, one that's our own."

She smiled. "Maybe we can save that for after we get married," she said softly.

"Why?" I asked, curious. "We spend every night together at the apartment. I want us to have our own place as soon as possible."

She smiled but didn't reply, glancing away at the scenery.

"Hey," I said and kissed her knuckles again. "What are you thinking? Tell me."

She shrugged. "I just got my apartment," she said. "I don't want to give it up just yet. It's good to have a place of my own. You know, until we actually do get married."

I looked back at the road, pondering this development. She was reluctant to move in with me before we were married. Was it old fashioned or was it fear of being left at the altar again?

"Whatever makes you happy," I said softly, squeezing her hand.

"When we set a date, we can start looking for a place for after we're married. How does that sound?"

"It sounds perfect," I said.

Perhaps I was rushing things with Ella. We had only known each other for less than four months, but we'd been very intense for most of that time. I didn't want to be apart from her if I could help it.

We drove up to her parent's place in Concord. Bridges House was a stately old Colonial two-story mansion set on eleven acres of land north of the city. Built in 1836, it had long been the Governor's residence. It smacked of history, and I looked forward to staying there, just to soak up some of my country's past.

As I drove up, Ella took my hand and squeezed. "Just relax. My dad is intense, but he knows how to make conversation, too. He's had a lot of years in politics and can BS along with the best."

"I'll try," I said, my voice cracking with mock fear.

Ella laughed and leaned over, giving me a kiss before we got out of the car. I went to the trunk and removed our suitcases, while Ella waited for me. Then, we went to the front door together and I cleared my throat so that the first words out of my mouth sounded strong and confident.

In other words, not a croak.

I didn't know Governor Carlson, but I knew one thing: he wouldn't respect me if I croaked at him or sounded the least bit hesitant.

The door opened before we even got to it and Ella's mother was there to welcome us, her arms open.

"There you are, you two!" she said, her voice full of emotion. "We're so glad you could make it. Come in, come in! Emmet is in the living room on the phone to someone or other." She gave Ella a big hug and kiss, and then came to me and gave me a big warm hug, too. When she was finished, she stood back and glanced over me, her gaze moving over me from head to foot. "You're taller than I imagined."

I smiled. "I sprung up when I was thirteen and was always the gawky teenage boy whose head was above the crowd."

"Well, you certainly grew into your height," Ella's mother said, her eyes wide. Ella gave me an exasperated look and I laughed, taking it as a compliment.

I put the bags down and removed my coat and boots, watching while Mrs. Carlson and Ella went into the living room from the entry. The house was beautifully kept up, the furniture all 18th and 19th-Century antiques, the paneling warm. A huge fir tree dressed in gold and burgundy with white lights stood in the entry and gave the space a fresh pine scent.

Ella came back and waved me in. "Come," she said. "My father is in his office right now taking a call. The coast is clear. I'll take you to your room."

"Okay," I said and adjusted my sweater. "Do you think I'll pass muster?"

She grabbed my hand and laughed. "If anyone can, you can."

She led me upstairs to the second floor and to a bedroom at the rear of the building. It was pretty small but still, very nice by any standard. I laid my suitcase on the bed and grabbed Ella, taking the opportunity to get in a kiss before we had to go back down to face the parents.

Ella slipped her arms around my shoulders and tilted her head to one side. "My mother thinks you're a hunk. I have to agree."

"Oh, yeah?" I said, smiling. "I just hope your father thinks I'm more than a hunk of you know what."

"Don't be silly. You're amazing."

"No, you're amazing," I said and kissed her again. "I wish my father could have met you. I think my mother would have definitely liked you. She was her own woman, even for her day so she would have seen herself in you."

Ella sighed. "I wish I could have met them, too. I feel so lucky that I have both my parents. Yours had such bad luck."

"I know. I hope I can escape the Macintyre bad genes for cancer."

We embraced, and I felt bad that she'd never know my parents, but at least in a couple of days, she'd get to meet my brothers. All of them.

I knew they'd love her, too.

W e went to the living room and I walked around the room, taking in its splendor. The architects and decorators took great care to retain the old character of the house, upgrading where it made sense, but keeping everything stately, as was fitting for a Governor's Residence. Other than official paintings and decor, there was a small part of one wall set aside for the Governor's personal family photos, and I got to see pictures of Ella as a child, and then when she was older, taken in various locations. As an only child, she would have had all the attention of two very well-educated parents. No wonder she was headstrong.

"I was such a geeky kid," she said when she came to my side, taking my arm. "My mom taught high school English and encouraged me in my dreams to become a writer or editor at a publishing house."

"You're lucky. A lot of parents discourage their kids from the arts, out of fear they won't be able to earn a living."

"I'm not doing so well yet," she said with a laugh. "Unpaid internship and all."

"That's the way to get inside," I replied, taking her hand in mine. "That way, the people not paying you will learn your character and skills and will be willing to risk hiring you for pay. A credential such as a degree or certificate often isn't enough to know if someone will fit into your organization and be a good employee."

"That's why I did it," Ella replied. "I could have got a job at some random company writing copy for ads, but I want to be a book editor. I want to be in publishing."

"Then you picked the right course of action," I said and bent down to kiss her. We pressed lips together, and I pulled her against me, enjoying the moment. Of course, it was at that precise moment that Governor Carlson picked to come into the living room.

He cleared his throat, and we quickly pulled apart. I caught Ella's eye and she had this look of oh, oh, now it starts...

Or maybe that was me.

You'd think, given that I had survived boot camp and four years of service that I'd be able to face on father of my fiancée, but you'd be wrong. At that moment in my life, pleasing Governor Carlson was the most important thing next to making Ella happy.

"So, I finally get to meet the mysterious Joshua Macintyre Jr," Governor Carlson said. He stood there, his hands on his hips and gave me the once over like he was assessing me. I knew I passed muster in a general masculine sense of one man assessing another. I was tall and well-built, handsome in a boyish way (or so I had been told) and was well-dressed. I had military service under my belt and a degree as well from a top university. I was worth millions and one day, maybe billions.

Yet, his assessment of me mattered a whole lot more because I knew my name and family had all this baggage with him that would predispose him against me.

I extended my hand. "Governor Carlson, I'm so honored to finally meet you."

He almost -- almost-- withheld his hand, but finally offered it and we shook, his grip very firm like he was testing me. I was taller than him by maybe two inches and a couple dozen pounds heavier, but of course, he was a governor of an important state in the Union and in some ways, was more important overall than me, despite my family's fortune and influence in the world of commerce.

"So, you're the son of the man who sent my partner to jail over some petty financial accounting mistake and a personal misunderstanding."

I was taken immediately aback by his words. It wasn't a petty financial accounting mistake. Not by a long shot. It was clear insider trading and an attempt to hide it after the fact.

My instinct was to throw it back into his face, because if he really believed that, he was wrong and needed to be better informed. If he knew that was a lie, he was outright lying to my face.

"Daddy, that had nothing to do with Josh," Ella said beside me, her grip on my arm tightening like she was afraid he and I would come to blows.

"Emmet, you promised," Mrs. Carlson said, grabbing his arm and squeezing. He gave her a glare and then turned back to me.

"I hope we can put all that behind us, Governor Carlson," I said and squeezed Ella. "Ella and I are in love and want to spend our lives together. I want us all to be on the best terms and it would really help if we could just let the past be the past. I had nothing to do with what happened and so I hope any responsibility for it rests with people who are no longer with us."

"Yes, Daddy, Josh's father only died a few months ago. Please, don't try to re-fight old feuds."

Finally, Governor Carlson held up his hands as if in surrender. "Okay, okay. I'll let it go. I just want you to know that I haven't forgiven your father for what happened. It destroyed my partner's career. He spent several years in prison."

I bit my tongue, not wanting to make things worse. I could have said that he stayed at what was like a luxury boarding school compared to normal prisons in the country and that he went back to his private world of wealth, with only his reputation, and not his bank account, tarnished, despite making a boatload of money from his transactions. While he had to forfeit that money and pay a hefty fine on top of his jail sentence, he still had a massive investment account that was unaffected by any of his fraudulent actions.

What alarmed me was that Governor Carlson, then the man's business partner, was never implicated in any of his crimes. He escaped closer scrutiny for some reason, and I suspected it was either that he was innocent and raised no red flags with investigators, or he was dirty as hell and bribed his way out of trouble.

I hoped it was the former and not the latter.

Ella grabbed my hand and pulled me away from the living room. "I'm going to give Josh a tour of the house," she said, her voice a bit shaky. "We'll get our rooms set up and meet you and Mom for a drink before supper. How does that sound?"

"Sounds perfect, sweetie," Mrs. Carlson said, visibly relaxing. She grabbed Governor Carlson's arm and pulled him in the opposite direction. "We're going to go check on supper and maybe Emmet will get us a nice bottle of wine from the wine cellar." She raised her eyebrows meaningfully at Governor Carlson and before we could respond, Ella had me into the hallway and towards the other side of the building.

"Oh, my *God*," Ella said, her voice exasperated. "I thought Mom would have whipped him into shape by now, but he's a stubborn man."

"He has a solid backbone, that's for sure," I replied, trying to let go of all the animosity I felt in reaction to Governor Carlson.

"It's made of steel," she replied with a light laugh.

"Give us time," I said and squeezed her hand. "The very last thing I want is trouble between your father and me. I wanted us to be respectful in our disagreements, if any, and on friendly terms. He's important to you and I want to be on better than friendly terms with him."

"Good," she said. "Someone has to back down between the two of you."

"I'm happy to be the one to back down," I replied. "For you. Because I love you and want us to be happy to spend time with your parents. I want your father to like and admire me. I'll be a good boy on my best behavior if it means I can get him to forget about the past."

"Thank you," she said and leaned her face up for a kiss, which I gave her gladly.

The way I figured it, the man was going to be my father-in-law -- the only father I would have for the rest of my life. He was a very respected man in politics, and I didn't want him on any side against me or mine. Christian was a professor of law and wanted to get into politics one day. I didn't want Governor Carlson to be an enemy in the federal party.

We did the tour through the house and Ella showed me the grand kitchen with its chef-level appliances, just like my house in Montauk. I imagined that given the heavy entertaining schedule a governor would have, they would need a professional kitchen, even if most of the food was catered. Next, we visited Governor Carlson's office which was all decorated in rich warm paneling and had a lovely fireplace and mantle with a portrait of some notable historic Governor hanging over the mantle.

Finally, she took me to the back patio, and we stood in the cold, our breaths visible on the cold air, and took in the property. It was a pretty nice old historic building.

"I know it can't compete with your family property in Yonkers, but it's nice."

"It's very nice," I said. "With deep historical significance. Money isn't the only measure of value."

"I know," she said and squeezed my arm, pulling me back inside. "It's just that I'm aware of how privileged you were, growing up. It must all seem pretty mundane to you."

"Not at all," I said and kissed her. "I have tremendous respect for the history of our nation and institutions. This is part of it."

We went into the kitchen where a tray of appetizers was laid out. Governor Carlson and Mrs. Carlson were busy getting glasses and the bottle ready. Governor Carlson even smiled at me when we entered the kitchen.

"Would you like some wine, or perhaps a bottle of beer?"

"Beer would be nice," I replied, preferring a beer over wine when given the choice.

He went to a small built-in chiller and pulled out a bottle of beer from some local craft brewery, which impressed me.

"Thanks," I said and removed the cap, placing it into the trash beside the counter. "I love a good craft beer."

"Me, as well," he replied. "I'll have one, too."

That was a good sign. He was at least trying to be friendly with me. Drinking beer with me was like a message that the two of us men could be on good terms.

At least, I hoped it was...

I watched while he opened the bottle of chilled white wine and poured a taste for Mrs. Carlson. She took it and smelled the wine's bouquet before taking some into her mouth. So, she was a wine aficionado. I'd have to remember that.

"It's nice," she said, and Governor Carlson poured two glasses for Ella and her mother.

For the next hour, we sat in the living room and listened to some jazz on the sound system, then talked about nothing important, carefully avoiding all talk of current politics. Instead, we talked about the weather, the stock market, my brothers and their various occupations, and of all things, Brexit. It was the closest we came to anything political. I was glad Governor Carlson was being a good boy. I did my very best to be one as well.

We had a very nice dinner, and then I was careful to drink the wine that he chose for the meal. I didn't know a great deal about wine, but it was clear that Ella's parents did and took pleasure in commenting on the wine and its quality and vintage.

Ella sat beside me and we held hands beneath the table, our legs touching.

Finally, after a delicious dessert, we went back to the living room and Governor Carlson played some Christmas music on the sound system and we opened one present each, which was a tradition in the family.

Luckily, I had made sure to buy something for both Governor Carlson and Mrs. Carlson, based on what Ella told me about each of them. I bought a biography of FDR for the Governor which was topping the charts at the time and which was published by none other than Macintyre Publishing. I bought a literary work for Mrs. Carlson -- one of her favorite authors. And for Ella, I gave a beautiful diamond necklace that had once been my mother's.

Both Ella's parents seemed pleased with their gifts from me, but it was the look in Ella's eyes when she saw my gift that made my night.

"Oh, Josh, you shouldn't have," she said and stared at the necklace. "The diamond is so huge."

"It was my mother's," I said softly. "She would have wanted you to wear it."

Ella held her hand over her heart "Oh, Josh…"

We kissed and I saw Mrs. Carlson smile, while Governor Carlson kept an impassive expression on his face.

It looked like our two days stay in Concord might turn out all right.

3

ELLA

OUR STAY IN CONCORD TURNED OUT BETTER THAN I expected. Besides the initial moment when my father behaved badly towards Josh, bringing up the past with his father, they got along quite well. Christmas morning, we opened the rest of our gifts and had a nice brunch, and then did nothing but watch old movies for the rest of the day until it was time for Christmas Dinner. My father had invited some of his friends over for dinner and so we all got dressed up in our best clothes and spent an hour before dinner having cocktails with the invited guests, and then a very delicious meal of roast turkey and all the trimmings.

Josh and I sat beside each other so I could talk to him when the conversation lagged, just in case, but he didn't need much help. He had quite an animated discussion with one of my father's best friends about the military, even getting down to the nitty gritty about troop deployments in the Middle East, and America's role as the police force for the world. At times, I worried that the discussion would get too political, but luckily, they were all on the same page politically and about the military and so it was a good discussion instead of one that devolved into a battle.

After the guests finally left close to midnight, we all went up to bed and I kissed Josh at his door, winking at him that I'd try to sneak in during the middle of the night if I was able to wake up enough.

"Don't worry," he said and ran his thumb over my cheek. "We'll be together at David's place. Have a good sleep. I'll see you in the morning. We have to drive back to New York and catch our plane."

"Okay," I said and kissed him again.

Then I went to bed and slept like a proverbial log.

I n the morning, after I had a shower and dressed, I bumped into Josh on the stairs as he was coming up from the main floor.

"You up already?" I said and gave him a kiss.

"I went for a run," he replied and pulled me against him. "I thought you were going to sneak into my room last night," he said under his breath.

"But you said to wait until California," I protested.

"I didn't think you really meant that. I said it just in case your father was listening in."

"His room is on the other side of the building," I replied. "How could he listen in?"

Josh shrugged and squeezed me. "I don't know. The walls have ears? Haven't you heard that before? I was lying awake at 3 AM, hoping you'd sneak in for a quickie. I was crushed with disappointment when you never showed." He pushed his bottom lip out in a pout.

I frowned, for he really sounded like he meant it the previous night.

Then I saw the gleam in his eyes, and he laughed out loud. "Gotcha! Seriously, I meant it. I don't want to do anything to give your father an excuse not to like me. I'm going to be his only son-in-law, so I'll be a good boy, even if it means I don't get to indulge in you the way I want. I can wait until we're married to sleep in the same bed with you when we're here."

I leaned into his arms and kissed him. "And that's part of what makes me love you so much."

We kissed again and then he let go. "Now, I need to go for a shower. I'll meet you in the kitchen for breakfast. It smells good whatever your mom is cooking."

"Oh, it's not Mom cooking. It's dad. He said he wanted to fix breakfast for us since we're leaving early. He usually cooks brunch every day after Christmas. Gives Mom a break. He does Eggs Benedict, fried potatoes, sausage, toast, the works."

"Good," Josh said. "I need the fuel to keep me going today."

He went upstairs and had a shower and I went down to the kitchen and watched my father fixing the Hollandaise sauce.

"So, this young man of yours," my father said as he whisked the sauce over the double boiler. "You love him?"

"Of course, I do," I said, watching his face. "I wouldn't be marrying him if I didn't. After what I went through with Derek, I'm once bitten twice shy, but Josh is such a good man. He's really good, Father."

"I think so," my father replied. "My friends were impressed with him, and that counts for a lot in my books. Sorry that I was a bit harsh when we first met."

"That's okay," I said and leaned up to kiss him on the cheek. "I know that you're really sensitive about it."

"We'll just put it all behind us and move on," he replied. "As long as you're happy, I'm happy."

"I am *very* happy."

"Then I am, too." He smiled and then turned back to his sauce, which was done. "There," he said, holding up the whisk to show how nicely thick the sauce was. "Perfection."

We had breakfast, and it went just as well as had the previous day and night, so when it came time to leave, I really wished we could stay longer.

At the door, as we got on our coats and boots and prepared to leave, I felt all teary-eyed that I wouldn't see my parents again for a while. My hopes for the time spent with them were more than met, and even exceeded because I had feared that Josh and my father would get into an argument over the past.

Luckily, both Mom and I worked on my father enough for him to leave it all behind.

"Take care of my only girl," my father said to Josh as they shook hands goodbye.

"You can rest assured I will, Sir," he said to my father. Using the formal "Sir" was just the right choice, showing my father due respect and deference, plus letting him know he needed to "take care" of me. I knew it was all man-speak that they had to get through before they could be at ease with each other. Hopefully, one day after we were married and settled down, Josh and my father would actually become closer.

Until then, a friendly detente was good enough for me.

I kissed and hugged my mom and so did Josh, and we left.

After we got into the car and drove off, Josh turned to me, a smile on his face.

"That went well, I think," he said. "There were no pistols at dawn, so I'd say the stay was a success."

"A clear success," I said and squeezed his hand. "Now, I hope I can impress your brothers as much as you impressed my parents."

"Just be your sweet smart self and they'll be eating out of your hand."

O ur trip to California was unremarkable, except for the crowds at the airports both at JFK and LAX. Our drive to the mansion was quite emotional as Josh talked about the accident and how David was doing. David managed to get the EP finished and ready for mixing, so that was good. David had been able to overcome his sadness over the death of his friend, and they'd lucked into finding a new band member to replace Terry.

By the time we arrived, it was late, and we were both tired. I was excited, however, and a bit anxious to meet all the brothers. Hopefully, most of them would be in bed and I'd get away with just meeting David.

No such luck. Everyone was still up and standing around in the kitchen when we pulled up. David must have been waiting for us because he was there, waiting at the door for us, even coming down to open my door for me before I could get my seat belt off.

"There you are, future sis-in-law!" he said and grabbed me when I got out of the car. "Give me a big hug."

I laughed and we hugged, then he pulled back and looked me over. "You're as pretty as the picture Josh showed me. You have to come inside and meet everyone else. We're all dying to meet you, see who snagged our big brother."

"Hey, give the poor woman a chance to get her coat off."

David led me inside and helped me get my coat off while Josh brought in our suitcases. The house was out of this world. The circular entry was a full two stories high and as big as my entire dorm room back in New Hampshire. It was marble and glass with a beautiful water treatment by the door, the water falling and making a pleasant sound.

"Wow," I said and glanced around, waiting for Josh to join me. "This is amazing."

"It's a bit ostentatious, but that's what LA is all about, isn't it?" David said and gave Josh a big hug, the two men looking in each other's eyes meaningfully. "How are you, bro?"

"I'm fine," Josh replied. "The question is, how are you?"

The way Josh said it suggested he was worried about David and by the expression on his face, I knew he was.

"I'm great," David said, his tone dismissive of Josh's obvious concern. "Couldn't be better, in fact. We finished up the EP, and my manager is busy working on a schedule for our world tour starting in July. It's going to be a great year."

He patted Josh on the back as if to assuage Josh's fears for him, and then grabbed each of us by one arm, escorting us into the mansion. I could hear sound coming from a distant part of the building, and we emerged into a large living room, with three different sitting areas, and huge glass doors leading out onto a massive patio with large lights and a pool.

"Here they are!" David said, his voice ebullient. "The happy bride-and-groom-to-be!"

We went over to the small group of whom I assumed were Josh's siblings and they were a very handsome and well-turned out group. I felt a bit self-conscious as the only woman there, but I took in a deep breath and smiled, preparing to meet each one.

I was still a bit in awe of David, for he was perhaps the best known of the brothers because of his success as the singer for the metal band Ranger. Tall, longish dark hair and blue eyes, a goatee and tattoos all down his arms, he was handsome in a dangerous way. There was a gleam in his eye, and you expected that he'd tease you at any moment. He was also muscular in contrast to what I usually expected from musicians, who I tended to think were lean instead of built. But everything else was what I expected for a metal front man -- leather jeans, a tight black t-shirt with the logo for

Ranger on it and the figure of a tall man in a long coat — the symbol for the band.

Named after Aragorn, in Lord of the Rings, who was a Ranger, the band was a mix of prog rock and metal and influenced by the classic prog rock bands from the 70s and beyond as well as Metallica and classic metal bands. It wasn't my cup of tea when it came to music, but I could recognize that they were good -- very good -- at what they did. They had a big fan base.

"Hey, brother," one of the men said and embraced Josh. "Good to see you."

He hugged each brother in turn and then when he was finished, he turned to me, smiling.

"And this," Josh said and pulled me closer to him, one arm going around my shoulder. "This is the love of my life, my wife-to-be, Ella Carlson. Ella, I present to you my brothers."

Then he introduced the other brothers to me, and there wasn't a better-looking group of men around. Each one was handsome in his own right, from Nash, the former fighter pilot who now ran a small airline with his dark hair and amber-brown eyes, to Christian, whose hair was lighter and who looked like a model on some Armani runway, to Michael, who had very stylish short black hair and intense blue eyes, a well-trimmed beard. All were tall, and all were well-built, dressed in expensive but casual clothes.

It could have been a meeting of male models, instead of a family get together.

By the time introductions were over, I felt a need to escape but instead, I spent the next hour sitting in the middle of them all on the patio, the lights of LA spread out beneath us, and listened to them talk. They kept asking me questions and ribbing Josh about him always being the first to do everything -- to join the military, to graduate with a degree, to be engaged -- *twice*.

"We hope this one sticks," David said and smiled at Josh. Beside him, Nash punched David's shoulder.

"David," he said. "For God's sake. Don't mention it."

"Aw come on," David said with a laugh. "I was just lightening the mood. I know Josh is in love. I could tell back when he talked to me on the phone about coming out here to open the new office of MBC."

David smiled at me. "Glad to have you here sis. Welcome to the family."

I smiled, because I could tell there was a lot of love between the brothers and that had to be a good thing. I turned and squeezed Josh's hand, glad that while I had been an only child growing up, I would finally have four brothers.

At that moment, despite being a bit overwhelmed by all the attention, and feeling like I needed to catch my breath, I couldn't be happier.

4

JOSH

"Hey, guys, hold up," I said when my brothers eagerly crowded around Ella and peppered her with praise and questions about me and our relationship. She looked overwhelmed for a moment and I wanted to give her some breathing space. "Let Ella have a few moments to catch her breath, okay?"

They laughed and stepped back, and I pulled Ella into my arms.

"I was an only child," Ella said, "so I'm so happy to be getting a bunch of brothers in the deal."

That was the perfect thing for her to say, and I knew it would endear her with them.

"We all wanted a sister when we were young but each time my mother gave birth, it was another brother," Christian said.

"You were disappointed in me?" Michael said, giving Nash a playful punch on the shoulder.

"Naw," Nash replied, squeezing Michael's shoulder. "I had someone to push around for a change, instead of being pushed around by Josh."

"So that's how it was with all of you," Ella said, smiling. She turned to David. "You were the youngest. Who did you push around?"

"Our dog Charlie," David said with a laugh.

"It's true," Nash said. "Charlie was the best-trained dog we ever had. We all thought David would become a vet, but he picked up a guitar and that was it. He forgot about veterinary college and went after the money for nothing and the free chicks."

"You got it," David said and laughed.

I turned to Ella. "Let's go take our suitcases upstairs and then we can come down and have a drink with the brothers."

"Sounds good," Ella said, her expression telling me she was glad to have a moment's break from the inquisition.

I grabbed both our suitcases and Ella followed me upstairs to the second-floor wing where the guest bedrooms were located.

"This is ours," I said and opened the door to our room.

The bedroom David had prepared for us was huge and had a magnificent four poster king sized bed in the center. Behind it was a pair of patio doors that led to a balcony looking out over the LA vista. Ella checked the place out, including a huge en suite bathroom with a jet tub and stand-up two-person shower.

"The view is amazing!" Ella said and went to open the patio doors while I laid the suitcases on the bench at the foot of the bed.

I followed her out and put my arms around her from behind, resting my chin on the top of her head.

"It is nice," I said. "It's so quiet out here. There's no city noise and I like it, but I can still see the city."

"I could get used to it," Ella said, squeezing my arms around her waist. "But I'd feel so far away from everyone."

"I know what you mean," I said. "But the flight is only a few hours. We could fly here and back easily if we wanted. We could live here in the winter, and in Manhattan in the summer."

"That would be nice," she replied and turned around in my arms. We kissed, the kiss starting out soft but deepening.

"Mmm," I murmured against her throat when the kiss broke. "You're going to get me all randy and I won't want us to go back and socialize with my brothers..."

"We can't do that," she replied with a coy look in her eyes. "I want to talk to them, get all the dirt on you when you were growing up."

"There's no dirt to get, I'm afraid," I said in mock sadness. "I was the good brother who did the right thing. I never broke the rules."

I glanced down at her to see if she believed me, but she narrowed her eyes.

I laughed, and that ended my attempt to appear serious.

"I highly doubt you were a saint when you were growing up. You have bedroom eyes, so I bet you got a lot of girls into your bed with them."

"Bedroom eyes?" I said, innocently. "What could you mean, Ms. Carlson? What would your father think of you talking like that?"

She leaned up on her tip-toes and kissed me quickly. "He'd threaten to wash my mouth out with soap, that's what he'd do."

"Really?"

"I'd be grounded and forced to do the grunt work for the week."

"Grunt work? Your father was in the military, right?"

"Briefly," she replied.

"What grunt work would you do?"

"Take out the garbage, rake leaves, vacuum. That kind of thing. Once, I called him a sonofabitch when we had a fight and he said that if I was going to swear like a trooper, I'd have to work like one."

I laughed at that, imagining Governor Carlson frowning at a younger Ella after she swore at him. "You called the Governor a sonofabitch?"

"I did," she replied and smiled. "He wouldn't let me go out to a party on a Saturday night because I was late getting home the night before. I felt he was being unreasonable and too strict."

I nodded, understanding that Ella had been a bit rebellious as a girl.

"You had to do all his chores for the week?"

She nodded. "I used to come home from school and read what I had to do on the chalkboard in the kitchen. Every day for a week, he'd have a grunt-work chore for me to complete. You can be sure I didn't call him a swear word again. But I did learn how to rake and mow a lawn, how to take out the trash and do other things around the house that he usually did."

"So, he did you a favor," I replied

"That's the way he saw it," Ella said. "He taught me the value of holding my tongue when faced with an authority who could punish me. I tend to keep my mouth shut in those cases."

"Good lesson," I said. "Shall we go downstairs and join the brothers?"

"Yes," she said and squeezed me. "We can continue this later."

"We most definitely will," I replied giving her butt a soft smack as she led the way.

We had a nice time sitting on the patio with the brothers, and by the time midnight came around, Ella yawned and gave me a look that suggested she'd had enough for one night.

"I'm afraid I have to take my bride-to-be and go to bed," I said and stood, holding out my hand to her. "We've had a busy couple of days, traveling and visiting the parental units, so we need the sleep."

"Okay, bro," David said and stood, coming over and giving me a hug. "Thanks for coming. Both of you. I'm so happy to have everyone here this year. Our first year as complete orphans."

"Aww," Ella said, and pouted. "I'm sorry. This isn't a happy time for you, I guess."

"No, I'm fine," David said and gave Ella a hug and kiss on her cheek. "It's just the first time we've all been here for the holidays instead of in Manhattan and it feels different. It wasn't a traditional Christmas without Dad."

"We have to make our own traditions now," Josh said and nodded. "Maybe we'll alternate Christmas in Manhattan and in LA. How does that sound?"

"Sounds perfect," David said.

We all hugged and kissed again and then I took Ella back up to our bedroom.

"That's so sad," she said when we were in the bathroom, brushing our teeth, she in her tiny nightgown and me in my boxer briefs. "Your first year without your dad. I can't imagine not having my mom and dad around."

"It's hard," I said and rinsed my mouth out. "I have to be the head of the family now."

"You do it well," she replied and smiled.

I smiled back, but I wasn't so sure. I was the CEO of MBC, but my father had his own authoritative presence that I knew I'd never have nor would I want. I just wanted to be a brother. We were all men, now, and so we were more of a tribe with no chief instead of the way it was with my father. Ella was lucky to still have both her parents alive and within a few hours of Manhattan. I was determined that I would be on good terms with Governor Carlson and Ella's mom.

I wanted them to become my surrogate parents. I wanted to feel love for them both someday. At that point in our relationship, they were still strangers, although Ella had told me enough about each of them that I had a pretty good picture of them as parents in my mind's eye. But I didn't feel any emotion for them yet except the regular amount of respect for my elders. I hoped that changed soon after we married. I wanted a very happy and fulfilling family life with Ella.

The kind of life my own father had with my mother and with us boys. A sense of sadness filled me at the thought of losing my dad too soon and I took in a deep breath and tried to chase it away with thoughts of visiting the beach with Ella during our trip.

When we were finished getting ready for bed, Ella slipped her arms around my neck and kissed me tenderly.

That was the last time I thought about my sadness over my father's death for the rest of the night.

The next morning, we spent time on the patio eating our breakfast al fresco, and then I turned to my brothers.

"What's on for the day?"

"I plan on lying by the pool," Nash said. "Whenever I can enjoy the sun in December, I try to take full advantage of the quiet. I've been working like a dog and need peace and quiet."

"What about you guys?" I asked the other brothers.

"We're going to hang around and soak up the sun with Nash," Michael said.

Christian nodded. "Me, three."

"What about you, David?" I asked, turning to him.

"I'm doing some work in the studio to polish the video for our website. You two kids go out and have fun."

I turned to Ella. "Feel like taking a drive to the beach?"

"I thought you'd never ask," Ella replied, a big smile on her face.

"You've never been to LA?" David asked, his eyes wide.

Ella shook her head. "Nope. The farthest west I've been was to Colorado."

"Oh, man, you're in for a treat," David said. He turned to me. "You should take her to Venice Beach and show her the sights."

"I will," I said and stood up from my lawn chair. "We'll get some fish tacos for lunch and watch the body builders bulk up. How does that sound?" I held out my hand to Ella and she took it and stood up.

"Sounds wonderful."

We left the brothers and took the rental car to the beach. On the way, we passed the site of the accident and I stopped the car for a moment, needing some time to revisit the whole event.

"Why are we stopping?" Ella asked, glancing over at me.

"This is where it happened," I said quietly and pointed to the side of the road where the SUV had rolled onto its side after the collision. We were on the opposite side and I could still see where the front end had hit the cement embankment.

"Oh, Josh..." Ella reached over and took my hand in hers. "I'm so sorry. We should have taken a different route."

"No," I said and smiled at her. "I wanted to drive by and remember it."

"Why? I'd think you'd want to avoid it."

I shook my head. "It reminds me of how damn lucky I am to still be alive." I kissed her knuckles and then leaned over and kissed her mouth, my emotions building. "Maybe seeing it again will chase away some of the ghosts from that night and I won't wake up in the middle of the night in a cold sweat."

"You need counseling to help you get over it, Josh," Ella said softly. "It was a traumatic event. Someone you knew died."

"I barely knew Terry," I said. "I lost more men in Afghanistan."

"Your own life was at risk, though," Ella added. "And your brother was seriously injured. It was traumatic and you probably have PTSD to some degree. You should talk to someone."

I nodded, knowing she was right, but not liking to admit I couldn't handle it. That was stupid. I would be advising someone in my shoes to get some counseling.

"You're right," I said and kissed her knuckles again. "When we get back, I will see a therapist."

"You promise?"

I nodded. "I promise."

Then, we drove off and I watched the scene disappear in my rear-view mirror, glad that I'd stopped by, and happy once more to be alive and with Ella.

"Thanks for taking me there," she said softly.

"Why?"

"Because it shows me that you're letting me in," she said.

"I want you in," I said and squeezed her hand. "All the way in."

She smiled and turned back to watch the road as we arrived at the coast.

5

ELLA

WE SPENT A FEW HOURS AT THE BEACH, WALKING HAND in hand along the sand and enjoying the sound of the waves and the bright sunshine. We actually did stop at one of the small food carts parked along the road that bordered the beach and ate fish tacos. They were delicious -- made all the better by the fresh air and sunshine.

Then, we drove back, taking a different route home so Josh didn't have to see the accident site again, arriving at the house later in the afternoon. Josh's brothers were still outside, talking and laughing, drinking a beer together. They were a handsome bunch, and any woman would be lucky to snag one of them for a husband. I gripped Josh's hand and leaned in close for a kiss as we walked out of the house, feeling a surge of appreciation that we met and fell in love.

"There they are -- the two lovebirds," David called out, raising his beer. "Pull up a chair, Ella. Josh, get your woman a drink and join us."

I smiled and joined the four brothers while Josh got me a beer.

"So, what did you think of Venice Beach? Did it live up to your expectations?" David asked, his expression eager to hear how the day went.

"It did," I said. "It was wonderful to be able to walk along the surf in December. I haven't been away from the cold at Christmas and New Years for ages. It's really nice."

"You guys should move here after you're married. Josh could work out of the LA office. We could have family dinners. You two going to start a family right away?"

I glanced at Josh. "We haven't got that far yet," I said and took the beer from him when he came over to where we were sitting. "We're planning to buy an apartment and fix it up, make it our own first."

"What about the house on Montauk? You two going to live there?" Nash asked.

Josh sat beside me and reached over to take my hand. "We like it, but it's not practical for us at the moment. We're both working and need to be close to Manhattan. I don't want to be commuting every day. Maybe one day, when we can work from home, it might be an idea."

"I still want you to come live here," David said. "The LA office could be a headquarters for MBC. There's nothing that says it has to be in Manhattan. You were bitching to me about the cold winters."

"We have to get married first," I said and laughed. "We'll see how things go. I sure could get used to the weather here."

"Me too," Josh said. "It would be nice."

We chatted until it was time for dinner. The brothers remarked on the latest news and weather and of course, sports. I avoided talk of politics as much as possible, but the brothers, being brothers, were eager to verbally spar with each other over their political choices. I kept my head down when the conversation moved to the current political news, and listened instead, not wanting to get involved. It wasn't that I didn't have my own political views and preferences, but I didn't want them to get in the way of friendship with my new brothers-in-law. At some point in the future, when we had already established a comfortable bond, I would be more open, but for now, I just smiled and listened, laughing when someone cracked a joke and keeping silent when they made a point I didn't agree with.

It was just better that way.

Dinner was great. David stood at the grill and cooked a variety of meats and some seafood, while Josh and Michael prepared a salad and garlic loaf. I did nothing but drink my beer and enjoy listening to David talk about his EP and upcoming tour with Christian and Nash.

While we were waiting for the food and Josh was inside fixing something for dinner, Christian sat beside me on the patio, his beer in hand.

"So, how did Josh and your dad get along? He told me he was worried that the old business between our father's news station and Garner, your father's business partner would come up and cause problems."

I was surprised that Josh talked about it with his brothers, but of course he would -- and of course he would be concerned. He had been eager to meet my parents but was worried my father would still hold a grudge. Which he did, of course.

"They did pretty well. When my father brought it up, both my mother and I shut it down pretty quick," I said with a laugh.

Christian smiled. "That's what Josh said. I'm glad to hear it. I'd like to mend fences between your father and my family. The Governor is renowned in our party for making things happen, so I'd like to meet him now that we're going to be relatives."

"I'm not so sure he's totally chastised but he's been given the word on not talking about it. At least, until after we're married," I said, grinning. "He still thinks what happened was unfair. I expect he'll think that until his grave, to tell the truth."

Christian nodded. "I can understand he felt bad for Garner, but it's clear that he broke the law and deserved what happened. Your dad is lucky he didn't get dragged down with him."

"My father was innocent," I said, frowning. "He had nothing to do with what Garner did."

"That may be true, but often, a business partner's crimes can destroy the business they both share."

"Garner was doing something completely outside of their business itself, so it never affected him."

"Good to hear," Christian said and took a sip of his beer. I had the sense he didn't believe me -- that he thought my father was probably involved but got off. It rankled, to be honest. I felt like arguing with him more but then Josh walked out of the house and joined us, sitting beside me and taking my hand.

"So, what have you two been talking about? Garner, I'll wager," Josh said and narrowed his eyes at Christian.

"As a matter of fact, we were," Christian said. "I want to meet Governor Carlson and wanted to make sure you two were on good terms first."

"We will be on good terms," Josh said with a nod. "I think both of us want this family relationship to work out and so we'll keep our lips zipped."

"I hear you," Christian said and smiled. They clinked beers together and took a drink. I was glad that conversation was over. Christian's comment that my father got off lucky, by not being charged with a crime bothered me. I'd have to talk to Josh about it later, but at that point in the day, I didn't want to discuss it further with Christian.

Luckily, the talk moved to sports, and I was able to zone out and keep a slight smile on my face. I wasn't a big sports fan, but I didn't want to appear totally in the dark, so I listened to them talk about the various teams they supported and the players they favored.

"Dinner is served," David called out from the grill. He held out two big platters of food, one with meat and one with seafood. We got up and went to the large dining table on the patio and ate another meal by torchlight.

"David, it's fantastic to be here and sitting outside eating a meal," I said when he passed me my plate.

"You like it Sis?" he said, clearly pleased. "You and Josh have an open invitation to come and stay. The room will always be ready for you. Come for a weekend, come for a week or a month. Even when I'm on tour, feel free to come and escape when you need it. The more the merrier I always say."

I smiled at him and raised my beer in salute. It would be nice to be able to come out here whenever Josh and I wanted. The view was fantastic, the house was amazing and the weather, perfect.

Josh leaned over and kissed me. "We'll be happy to come out here whenever we need a break from the cold and noise and crowds."

"We will."

We sat on the patio after we were finished eating for a couple of hours, talking about everything, the brothers reminiscing about previous Christmas and New Years with their father, and both parents before their mother died. I felt so sad for them that they were now without parents and hoped they all found partners and had their own families.

They were such a nice, decent group of professional men that I wanted the best for them.

After Christian bowed out for the night, Josh turned to me and squeezed my hand. "Tired?" he asked.

"Yes," I said, and squeezed back. "I feel so relaxed out here that I could sleep for twelve full hours."

"Let's go to bed," Josh replied and stood, pulling me up with him.

"Good night you two lovebirds," David said. "See you for brunch tomorrow. Eleven o'clock. I'll do omelets tomorrow so if you want one, be up for then."

"Sounds great," I said and squeezed David's shoulder as I walked by. "Good night."

The other brothers said goodnight and we left the patio and went back to our rooms on the second floor. Once the door was closed behind us, Josh pulled me into his arms and gave me a warm kiss.

"I thought they'd never want to stop talking," he said and kissed my neck. "I have plans for you, Ms. Carlson."

I smiled while Josh kissed my throat, the feel of his body pressed against mine warming me up immediately.

"You have so many plans," I murmured as he pulled down the shoulder of my sundress and kissed the top of my breast.

"I do, and all of them involve multiple orgasms on your part."

I laughed softly. "You are such a braggart," I said and gasped when his lips tugged at my rapidly hardening nipple.

"But I always deliver," he replied standing up and staring into my eyes.

"You do."

He did.

The rest of our stay was more of the same -- spending time on the beach, eating great Mexican food from taco trucks on the side of the road, watching the surfers ride the waves, and generally decompressing after the busy fall we'd both had.

On the day before New Year's Eve, after Josh and I had finished packing, we went downstairs for supper.

When we entered the patio where the brothers were sitting around waiting for some food to be delivered, David stood with his hands on his hips, a sad expression on his face.

"You guys won't change your minds and stay for New Year's Eve?" he asked.

Josh sat on a lawn chair beside me. "We have plans to go to Time's Square for New Year's Eve, so we have tickets home tomorrow."

"Aww, damn," David said. "I thought we could have fun and watch the fireworks from my favorite vantage point."

"I'm staying," Christian said. "I'll be glad to go with you and watch."

Nash nodded. "Me, too. I'll go back to Phoenix when I'm recovered from the hangover that I know I'll have New Year's Day."

"Good," David said, apparently not wanting to have his little family get together end. "I like to have my bros with me at this time of year. I hate to see you two go, but I understand the appeal of Time's Square on New Year's Eve. Cold blistering wind, drunken crowds, security threats, you know. All that fun stuff."

He put his lip out in a fake pout.

"Maybe next year," Josh said and turned to me. "We'll spend Christmas here and stay for New Year's Eve."

"That's music to my heart," David said. "You guys will be married by then, right?"

Josh turned to me, his eyebrows raised. "We haven't set a date yet, but whatever the case, we'll be here."

"Have the wedding here," David said, his expression excited. "I'll host it at my place. We have enough room for your family to come and stay. I'd love to meet the Governor."

"We'll keep it in mind," I said with a laugh, glad that David was so happy about our engagement and forthcoming wedding. "It would be nice to have a winter wedding in a summer climate."

I turned to Josh and he smiled. "Whatever you want, I'm happy."

I went to David and kissed his cheek, which made him smile. "Thanks for the offer. We'll talk and consider it. We've already thought about some place exotic like Bora Bora or somewhere else in French Polynesia."

"Oh, count me in, in that case," David said and clapped his hands with glee. "I love that place. Fantastic clear water. Weather is amazing."

I glanced at Josh and he smiled at me and kissed my knuckles.

"We'll let you know when we make a firm decision," he said.

After our meal, which was authentic Korean BBQ, and which I worried would give me indigestion, we said our goodbyes, hugs and kisses and promises of keeping in touch, we left.

"Seriously, you two fly to LA anytime you need to get away from the cold. My door is always open to you both and the bedroom will always be ready."

David and Josh hugged and kissed, and they had a moment together, their foreheads pressed against each other. They'd been through a life-altering event together and it had changed them both.

As we left the house and I turned back to see the brothers standing on the front entryway, I smiled. I had always felt I lost out as a child not having other siblings, and now I had four, with the possibility of four sisters-in-law on top of it.

I truly felt blessed.

6

JOSH

New Year's Eve in Times Square is an event of a lifetime if you're not from Manhattan, but for me, it was just a huge crowd of people, some of whom might be very drunk or intent on picking my pocket -- or worse. But Ella wanted to go and ring in the New Year surrounded by tens of thousands of others, so I felt I couldn't argue.

Reg wasn't happy, however. Before we left for LA, well in advance of the date, I'd spoken with him, wanting to arrange it so Ella could have her New York Ball Drop experience.

"It'll be nearly impossible to keep you safe if you insist on staying in the middle of the crowd," he said, rubbing his chin thoughtfully.

"What are our options?"

He shrugged. "You could spend the evening in one of the clubs or restaurants in the area and then go out for the dropping of the ball at midnight. We could provide several bodyguards who could surround you, go with you into the crowd. You could stay for the ball drop, and then leave, going back to the venue afterwards. Or you could watch it on a flatscreen. Pretty much every bar with one will show the ball drop at midnight."

"Ella really wants the experience," I said. "Do whatever you can to make it happen. Get us a seat at The View. It's a good location close to Times Square so it won't be a big deal to get down to street level to watch the ball drop, get us in, and then get us out." The View was a revolving restaurant at the 48th floor of the Marriott, its patrons the well-heeled, and wanting a view of Times Square while they ate or partied.

Reg nodded. "If that's what you want, that's the plan. I'll make it happen."

"Thanks," I said, and we shook.

So, when we arrived back in Manhattan and finished unpacking, we had to get dressed up and ready for our night on the town.

We both put on our best night-out-on-the-town outfits, me in a steel grey suit, black tie and white shirt, and Ella in a little black dress, hose and heels. Over top went our warmest coats, gloves and boots to protect us against the weather. Then, we were driven to The View near Time's Square where we would enjoy a dinner and drinks. When the time came, Reg and his crew would escort us to a spot where we could see the ball drop. It might not be in the middle of the crowd, but it would have to do.

I didn't want Mr. Fedora to show up and threaten either of us. I still had no idea who he was, but until I did, I took it as a threat to one or the other of us, or both of us.

Not the best end to one of the worst -- and best -- years of my life.

We sat at our table in 'The View' as it was called, sipping our champagne cocktails and admiring the scenery outside our window. The crystal was all polished, the silverware, too. Linen tablecloths, brass fixtures finished the decor. Suits were thousands of dollars each and the diamonds in the ears and on the fingers of the women were huge.

"I don't belong here," Ella said, glancing around at the other patrons.

"You do now," I said and wagged my eyebrows.

She smiled and took a sip of her cocktail.

"A lot happened to both of us this year," Ella said. "You lost your father, became CEO of MBC, and bought the *Chronicle*."

I took her hand. "And I met you." I kissed her knuckles tenderly. Then, I leaned over and kissed her as well. "But speaking of big years, how about you? You graduated with your degree, you and Jerkface split, you moved to Manhattan and landed a plum job with Macintyre Publishing with an office looking out over Fifth Avenue."

"And I met you," she said, mirroring my own words.

I kissed her again, feeling at that moment totally and completely happy. The only thing that could have made me happier was for my parents to still be alive to meet Ella. They would love her -- of that I was certain. She was sweet and smart and determined. She was also lovely on top of it and had a good family.

Both my mother and father would approve.

Of course, their approval wouldn't be necessary, but it would make it perfect.

It was then that I wanted to set a date -- the perfect way to end the year.

"When do you want to get married?" I asked, taking both her hands in mine and watching her face to see her response. "Should we do a June wedding and be traditional? Or do you want fall colors? Maybe a winter wedding in good old California?"

Ella shrugged. "I don't know. What do you prefer?"

"I thought a bride would be excited about planning her wedding."

She exhaled. "I was excited when I was engaged to Derek, and look where that got me?"

I frowned. "Ella, I want you to be excited for our wedding. What's holding you back?"

She hesitated. "We've only known each other for a short time, when you add it up. Maybe a longer engagement is wise -- to make up for it?"

I couldn't help but feel deflated at that, thinking she'd be as eager as I was to set the date.

"You feel you need more time?" I said, sitting back, unable to keep a slightly sour note out of my tone. "I'd marry you tomorrow."

She squeezed my hand. "I don't mean that," she said softly. "I've decided. I want to marry you. I'm just trying to be smart instead of stupid, like the last time I got engaged. It's just, isn't there some kind of traditional time period before you get married after you get engaged? Three months?"

"People get married in Vegas on the spot," I said. "There's no limit that I know of."

I shook my head, feeling the great evening sour right in front of my eyes.

I knew she was right. Both of us had made mistakes with our last choice of potential marriage partners. She was only trying to be rational about it, but at the same time, her hesitation made me feel a sense of gloom.

"But if you insist," I said, not willing to give up and let the evening deflate. "Three months wait would bring us to April and an Easter wedding sounds good to me, if you're going to make me wait." I gave her a crooked smile.

"Josh," she said and leaned in closer. "I love you. I want to live with you the rest of my life. We can wait three months to make sure all the plans are in place and it's perfect. That's all."

"I know," I said and kissed her softly. "I shouldn't be like that, but I want us to get married -- soon. As soon as we have it all figured out. Location. The wedding dress. Food. Music. You know -- everything both of us thought we'd be doing a year ago."

She leaned closer and kissed me. "Are we each other's consolation prize?"

"No," I said and cupped her cheek. "They were door number two. We're the real prize and thank God for jaywalking and the twist of fate that meant we found each other and finally picked the right door."

Then I kissed her with passion, my emotions getting the better of me. She kissed me back with just as much intensity. When the kiss broke, we looked in each other's eyes meaningfully.

"Easter sounds like a perfect time for a wedding," she said and smiled. In her eyes, I saw warmth and real happiness.

She had become everything to me. She was my heart and I didn't want to even imagine her being unsure or unhappy about our relationship.

"An Easter wedding sounds perfect," I said. "What do you say we have it in LA and make my little brother happy?"

She smiled. "It would make him happy, wouldn't it? He seemed so eager to have you or any of the brothers move to California. I think he's lonely."

"Losing Terry was hard on him," I said. "Losing his father and his best friend and bandmate in the same year was too much. I think it made him grow up a bit. He's always been one of those guys who never took anything seriously -- except his music. Losing Mom, then Dad and then Terry..."

"I can't imagine it," Ella said softly. "I never had siblings, and so I'm really happy to inherit a bunch of brothers."

"They're a great group," I replied, smiling at the thought of them. "You can expect to be spoiled and treated like a princess for the rest of your life."

"It works for me," she said with a grin. "You know us only children. Spoiled brats and lonely as hell, always dreaming of brothers and sisters..."

"Is that true?" I asked, curious. "I always had siblings -- an entire crew of brothers close in age. We played with each other and there was never a dull moment."

"You're so lucky," Ella said with a soft sigh. "I was pampered of course, but I was also lonely. I never wanted to have people over to my house. I always wanted to go to my friend's houses and be around their big families. When I saw people sitting around the dinner table at night, the noise and laughter, I was so envious. I wanted little sisters and a big brother and to have that kind of family."

"Well, now you have four big brothers."

"My cup runneth over," she replied, smiling, her eyes crinkling in the corners.

We kissed again, and when the kiss ended, I noticed a couple close to us watching us. They were smiling wistfully, probably remembering when they were our age and first in love.

It made me happy.

I leaned closer to Ella. "Don't look now, but we're making this older couple at the booth across the aisle really happy with all our snogging."

"Snogging?" she said and giggled. "Is that what you call it?"

"It's British," I said and wagged my eyebrows. "I'm an international man of refinement, didn't you know?"

"I didn't," she replied and leaned closer. "It sounds very unrefined. Probably not something the Queen would use."

"Probably not," I said and kissed her again. Then I saw her steal a look over at the couple, who were still watching us with fond remembrance. The woman smiled at us.

"Snog me again," Ella said. "Make them happy."

So I did.

A bout ten minutes to midnight, we asked our waitress if she could hold our table while we went out to watch the celebrations. I handed her a fifty-dollar bill as incentive and she took it and tucked it into her apron.

"It's yours as long as we're open."

Then, we grabbed our coats at the coat check and left the club, taking the elevator down to the lobby, determined to make it out into the crowd so we could ring in the new year properly, surrounded by thousands of Manhattanites hugging and kissing.

I'd almost forgotten about our little entourage made up of Reg's three bodyguards, who surrounded us and helped push through the crowd so we could get into viewing distance of the famous ball so we could watch it drop. While we waited, I slipped my arm around a shivering Ella and pulled her close.

"This has been one of the best and worst years of my life," I said. "It would have been one of the worst, if not for you."

She smiled up at me, her eyes soft. "Aww, Josh. I'm sorry about your dad. And the crash. And your ex. But you did get the paper."

"And I met you."

We kissed briefly and then turned and counted down the seconds. When the countdown ended and we hit midnight, I pulled her fully into my arms and lifted her up, kissing her deeply. She wrapped her arms around my neck and kissed me back, just as deeply.

"I love you," I said when the kiss ended. "Happy New Year."

"I love you, too," she replied. "Happy New Year back at you."

"Here's to many more New Year's Eve celebrations to come. Say, sixty or so. Maybe more, if they discover the secrets of immortality in the next few decades."

She laughed and we kissed again and again while the crowds cheered and celebrated, and fireworks exploded around us.

"Let's get out of here," she whispered as the throng crushed us. "I'd like another drink and then maybe we can go back to the apartment."

I motioned to our bodyguards and they found a route through the crowd back to the restaurant, where we removed our coats and went back to the table. After we got another drink, we held hands across the table.

"So, what do you see for the next year, since we're officially in it now? What do you want to have happen?" I asked.

She smiled and considered for a moment before answering.

"I want us to keep getting closer," she said. "I want to get a paying job so I can hold up my side of the sky."

I laughed. "As soon as your internship is over, you have a paid position if you want it."

"I want it," she said. "I want to be independent. I know, I know," she said and made a face. "You're worth millions, but I still want to have a career and accomplish things."

"Of course," I said. "You want to become an editor. You want to write your chick lit novel."

"I do," she said. "I want to travel. I've only been on vacations with my parents and only in the US, Canada and Mexico. I want to go to Europe and Africa. Asia. I want to go around the world."

"I'll be only too happy to take you everywhere. I've been so busy for the last few years, trying to get caught up with MBC after I finished my service. I haven't really done any traveling. We should spend a couple of years seeing the world in between business meetings, of course."

I smiled, for the expression in her eyes was one of pure excitement and contentment.

The feeling was mutual.

7

ELLA

At twelve-thirty, Josh glanced at his watch and then turned to me. "How are you feeling? Want more champagne? Or do you want to go back to the apartment for some special Josh treatment?"

I narrowed my eyes, pretending it was a difficult decision just to tease him, but it was a pretty easy decision.

"Special Josh treatment? Or another glass of champagne? Let me see..."

Then I laughed and he did as well.

"Josh treatment it is," I said finally. "Besides, if I have another glass of that, I'll fall asleep before any of the Special Josh treatment is experienced or doled out."

"Well, we don't want that," he said and held his hand over the bottle. "No more champagne for you."

Luckily, the bottle was finished so there was no need to worry about me trying to drink more. I was feeling a bit bubbly but not too much to enjoy what I knew awaited me back home.

Josh paid the bill and then we left with our coats, taking the elevator back to the lobby. Our crew of bodyguards surrounded us as we made our way to the limo service at the back of the hotel. As we drove off, I couldn't help but be overwhelmed with how much my life had changed since that day in September when I tried to cross the street and Josh almost ran into me.

There I was, engaged to one of the handsomest richest bachelors in Manhattan, driving back to his apartment in a limo. It was a far cry from my first day in Manhattan when I saw the tiny hole in the wall that had been advertised as a 'one bedroom' apartment.

Because of the crowds, it took a while to get back to the apartment, but we spent our time kissing, so instead of dampening our mutual desire, the long ride only enhanced it. By the time we arrived, I felt wet and swollen, ready for Josh.

Josh thanked the driver and made sure to pass him a hefty tip, then we went to the elevator, nodding to the security guard and saying goodnight to our bodyguards, who checked out the elevator before we got inside.

We kissed all the way up in the elevator, not caring if the security guards in the back room were watching. When the elevator reached the penthouse floor, Josh broke the kiss, and I was already breathless, anticipating what would happen next.

Josh and I went right into the bedroom, throwing our coats off on the back of the sofa on the way there. I practically tripped when I removed my boots, and giggled, slinging my handbag onto the chair by the door, eager to go with him into the bedroom.

Josh pulled me inside, and wasted no time, pulling down the shoulder of my dress, kissing the side of my neck and down to my collarbone and the swell of my breast.

"Oh, *God*, I need you," he murmured against my skin. Then, he pushed me back towards the bed, steering me until I felt the bed against the back of my thighs.

Josh pulled the other side of my dress down, baring my black lace push-up bra. He stood and admired me for a moment, running his fingers along the tops of my breasts, making me shiver with delight and arousal.

I clenched my thighs together unconsciously in response.

He kissed me, his mouth moving down my neck to my breasts, which he bared, one at a time, licking the swell before covering my now-hardening nipple with his mouth. I groaned when he sucked, my eyes closing.

When I reached down to remove my dress completely, he grabbed my hand.

"Don't," he said and looked in my eyes. "I want to watch you do it slowly. Tease me."

I stopped, trying to imagine what he'd most like me to do.

"What do you want me to do?"

"Expose one breast completely."

When I did, he ran his fingers over the curve, stopping to stroke my nipple, taking it between his finger and thumb, rolling it to a hard peak.

"Now, the other," he said and watched while I complied. He seemed to enjoy me following his commands.

Both breasts were now fully exposed, and I stood waiting for his next command, my body so in need of his touch. He cupped both breasts in his hands and bent down, kissing one and then the other, tonguing each nipple softly, then tugging hard.

I moaned, the sensations sending a zing of desire through my body.

"I love your breasts," he murmured against one. "I can't get enough."

He looked up into my eyes while he pulled down my dress. It fell into a puddle of fabric on the floor and I was left standing with my bra pulled down, my breasts exposed and my lacy black thong all that I had on.

"Beautiful," he said, standing back, admiring me.

I felt exposed but very wanton at that moment. His eyes on me, the possession in them, the lust, made me almost weak. It had been a long time since I felt such a mix of love and lust from a man -- maybe never. It made me need Josh's touch even more.

"You're perfect." He ran a hand down my body from my breast to my hip and then stepped closer, slipping his hand between my thighs. "*Mmm.* You're nice and wet."

"It's all your fault," I said with a coy smile.

He smiled back. "This isn't going to take long, is it?"

I shook my head.

Then he pushed me back onto the bed and I lay there, waiting, wondering what he'd do next.

He remained standing but removed his jacket and loosened his tie.

"Take off your thong," he said. When I reached down to remove it, he added, "Slowly."

I smiled to myself and tried to be as seductive as I could be, slipping the thin piece of lacy fabric down over my hips and then pulling it off my legs. He watched with obviously interest, his erection visible, pressed against his slacks. When I had the thong almost all the way off, I removed one foot and spread my thighs, knowing that would give him a good view of me. His eyes widened greedily in response.

Finally, I held the thong in one hand, my thighs spread, feet on the edge of the bed. I threw the thong over at the closet and waited for what Josh would do next.

"You're beautiful," he said in a throaty voice. "Perfect."

I smiled and closed my eyes, knowing I wasn't but glad he thought so anyway.

While I watched, he unfastened his belt and unzipped his slacks, letting them fall to the ground, before stepping out of them. Next, he removed his shirt and threw it aside, leaving him almost naked in his black boxer briefs, his erection straining against the fabric.

When he pulled them down, his erection, thick and red, sprung loose and the sight of it sent a jolt of lust through me, imagining how good it would feel when fully inside of me.

He climbed on top of me, leaning over my body, his knees between my thighs, which I spread even wider. He kissed me hungrily, and then began to devour the rest of me – his mouth moving over my chin to my neck, then each shoulder, his tongue tracing a line down between my breasts to each nipple.

When he got to my hips, he slid his fingers between my folds, spreading me wide.

"You're so wet," he said. "And ready."

He licked me slowly, up and down over my clit, until I was breathing rapidly, aching to feel him enter me and start to thrust. I needed to feel him inside of me but waited to see what he would do.

He slipped two fingers inside me and stroked while he licked.

"If you keep that up, I'm going to come," I said, my eyes closed.

"That's the idea..."

"I want you come with you inside of me," I said, my voice shaky.

"You will," he said. "We have all night."

I smiled. "Braggart."

"I deliver, so it's just truth in advertising."

Then I let myself go. He wanted me to come while he licked me and then make me come again while he fucked me.

It sounded like a great idea.

He continued to lick me, stroking his fingers inside of me while he did and soon, I felt my orgasm build, my body going over the line between pleasure and ecstasy.

"Oh, God," I said and tensed, my muscles all contracting as I orgasmed, my body clenching around his fingers.

He didn't stop, his tongue circling my clit until it was too much.

"Stop," I said, my voice shaky. "It's too much..."

Finally, he did, and my body recovered, my breathing slowing.

I lay still, recovering, and waited for what he'd do next.

He climbed on top of me and loomed over me, his erection in hand.

"Suck me," he said, I leaned up on my elbows, taking the head of his cock in my mouth, tonguing the rim and licking off the salty fluid that leaked out.

He closed his eyes, enjoying the sensation, but I knew he couldn't keep them closed. He loved to watch me suck his cock and so I did, sitting fully up, taking his cock in one hand stroking as I licked and sucked the head.

"That's good," he said, his voice deep. "That's so good..."

I sucked and stroked for a few moments and he watched, one hand on the wall behind us, the other on my head, guiding me gently.

His erection was rock hard, and I knew he was ready.

"Stop," he said and pulled away. "I want to come inside of you."

I pulled off his cock and waited for what he wanted to do next.

"Lie back," he said and so I did, spreading my thighs and lying back. He leaned over me, one hand sliding along my body, his fingers finding my clit. He stroked me again, then licked me before rising up and leaning over to the side of the bed for a condom.

While he removed it and rolled it over his cock, I waited, my body swollen and ready. I groaned with pleasure when he slid the head of his cock against my clit. When he pushed inside of me, I closed my eyes, enjoying the sensation of being filled completely.

He began thrusting slowly, completely withdrawing and then entering me again. Each time, the head of his cock rubbed the most sensitive spot inside of me. He knew exactly what I needed and soon, I felt the buildup of sensation and I knew I'd come after a few more thrusts.

"I'm going to come," I said, breathing hard. Josh began to thrust more quickly, pumping faster. My orgasm began, and I clenched around him through it.

"Oh, God, oh *God*," I cried out, my body spasming around him. In response, he thrust harder, and I knew he wanted to come when I did. Before my orgasm had waned completely, he groaned, and I saw him straining above me, his face contorted with pleasure.

When his orgasm finished, he collapsed on top of me.

"God, that was *good*," he said, his mouth beside my ear.

"It's always good," I said with a smile.

It always was.

"It was perfect," he murmured against my neck. I could hear the amusement in his voice.

"It was," I replied, closing my eyes and lifting my arms over my head, enjoying the moment.

It was the perfect way to start the year together.

After we cleaned up, we snuggled together, naked still, our arms around each other, the covers pulled up around us so that we were almost covered. It felt like our cocoon against the rest of the world and we two were all that mattered.

8

JOSH

Ella and I spent the next week off from work searching for a new apartment that we could call our own.

When I was engaged to Christie, we had planned to live in the penthouse my father owned on Central Park West, with a stunning view of Central Park. After the engagement was called off, I never wanted to set foot in the apartment, despite how perfect it would be for me. Instead, Christian got it in the will and for that, I was happy. He didn't have bad memories of it, so he could live there -- if he wanted -- and raise a family there in the future.

Ella and I wanted something that would be good for us as a new couple -- with at least two bedrooms, preferably three, so we could both have an office and a master bedroom. Since money was no object, we decided to buy something close to the Macintyre building on 5th Avenue.

There were a few properties we were interested in and arranged viewings the week before we went back to work. Of course, Ella was shocked at the price of the apartments, because she was used to properties in New Hampshire, which were much more affordable than those in Manhattan. You got so much less for your money -- but of course, that was the price people paid for living in one of the most prestigious neighborhoods in the entire USA.

After viewing about seven properties, all in the Central Park area, we settled on three and had to decide among them.

One penthouse apartment near was perfect and had everything on our list, including a roof-top patio for summer barbecues. Completely modern in decor and design, it was my pick for it looked brand new, with sparkling new appliances, and four bedrooms. It would mean we could each have an office and a guest bedroom for visitors -- or a baby.

Ella also liked a penthouse apartment that was more traditional with more of a Victorian design and decor. Everything looked like it was out of a 18th or 19th Century apartment in London or Paris. Also four bedrooms, it had a totally different character than the apartment I preferred. In the end, if Ella was happy, I'd be happy, so I told her that the choice was up to her. The price was close -- within a couple of million dollars -- and so it really didn't matter to me as long as we had what we needed.

The only other choice was for us to buy in an old building that was being renovated and design the apartment from top to bottom. It would be less expensive to buy but would require a few months of renovations before we could move in. We stood in the old apartment on the day of our viewing and tried to imagine what we would do with the place. Whoever owned it before had rented the apartment out for most of the past three decades and it was not kept up to date with appliances or paint, flooring. But it was a totally blank canvas.

We could make it completely our own.

"What do you think?" Ella asked me, taking my hand and squeezing. "Are we completely stupid to get this place and have to do all the work to get it the way we want?"

"No," I said. "That's Michael's business, building and renovating. I'm sure he'd love to take on the project and would make it perfect for us."

"Should we get him here to take a look at the place before we decide?"

I nodded. "Good idea. I'll call him and make an appointment for him to come and see it with us. We can talk about what we want done and he'll decide if it can be done."

We made another appointment and took a risk that our other choices would remain on the market for the time it took to see the fixer-upper with Michael. Luckily, he was available for a viewing the next afternoon.

Michael took his time looking at the place, inspecting all the fixtures and appliance hook-ups, and taking note of the layout and floor plan.

"Tell me what you want. I can do pretty much anything you like. The place needs new floors, new plaster, new fixtures, new appliances, paint, wallpaper. The bones are good, the layout is decent. You could open up the dining room and living room if you want a more open-concept layout. Or you can stick with the current plans and make it more formal and traditional."

I glanced at Ella, figuring she'd prefer the more traditional look. "Well?" I asked, squeezing her hand. "You like traditional."

"Would it bother you?" she asked, making a face of doubt. "I've always wanted a formal dining room where we could have big family meals. I don't want the kitchen and living room to be all one big mess."

"I'm fine with whatever makes you happiest." I bent down and kissed her to reinforce my words. Then I turned to Michael. "Traditional, it is. Maybe do some really nice plasterwork and antique fixtures. A professional kitchen with top of the line appliances and lots of space for cooking. One thing I do want to insist on is the view. I want to keep the huge picture windows that span the living areas, but maybe put new windows in that are more weatherproof and fit the decor. Maybe tall arched windows so we keep the traditional feel, but lots of light."

"Yes," Ella said and squeezed my hand. "I love the floor to ceiling windows in every room, but they need updating. Can you do that?"

"Everything's possible. What about the rooftop?"

We went upstairs to the rooftop area that came with the penthouse apartment. The building itself was only ten stories tall so we weren't up too high. There was nothing there and the space would have to be completely built anew.

"We want easy access from the apartment. We want a hot tub and a patio area with a covered barbecue. Plus, lots of planters for flowers. Maybe a more solid structure so we can spend a lot of time out there when the weather's nice."

"Sounds good to me," Michael said. "I can get a couple of my designers out to view the place and start plans as soon as you close the deal and have access. Renovations won't be too extensive, and I can probably get it done in a couple of months once we start."

"Great," I said and gave Ella a hug. "I can't wait to get started."

"Me, either. I never thought I'd be able to buy a place in Manhattan, let alone overlooking Central Park," she said. "It feels like I'm dreaming."

"It's not a dream," I said. "You'll have your own place. Hopefully, it will all be ready by the time we come back from our honeymoon. In the meantime, we'll have to pick out colors and fixtures, appliances and decor. You'll be kept busy."

"I'm up for the job," she said with a smile.

We went out for a drink with Michael after the viewing and caught up with him and his life. He'd always been his own man and had rebelled against my father's focus on politics and media. He was the kid who wanted the toy front end loader and tractor, spending his time in the sandbox at the playground digging holes and building sand forts. He went to university to study engineering but really liked carpentry and renovating old buildings. When he went into the military, he was part of the

Army Corps of Engineers. He liked to build things -- things that would last decades or even hundreds of years.

He enjoyed managing projects, taking them from the preliminary concept phase through to completion and was one of the most successful builders in Manhattan.

I had no doubt about how well his company was doing. What I wanted to know was how well his personal life was going and whether he was dating anyone seriously. I guess I wanted him to be as happy as I was.

"How's your love life?" I asked, getting right to the point. "Anyone in particular you're seeing or serious about? Last time I checked, you were unattached and happy to stay that way."

He shrugged. "I've got a few years of bachelorhood ahead of me, I figure. Dad's incentivized trust fund isn't going to encourage me either way."

"Oh, yeah," Ella said and turned to me. "I forgot about that. Is that why you're so eager to marry me?" she said with narrow eyes. "You want to get your first installment?"

My jaw dropped open at that and for a moment, I thought she was serious. Then I saw the corner of her mouth crook up in a barely suppressed grin.

"Oh, you," I said and bent down to kiss her. "You almost had me."

She finally laughed out loud. "Oh, the expression on your face was priceless," she said and turned to Michael. "Wasn't it?"

"It was," he replied and held up his beer in a toast. "You got him good."

It was while I was lifting my beer up to my lips that Jerome, one of our bodyguards, came over, bent down and whispered in my ear. Immediately, alarm bells went off in my head.

"Mr. Fedora's across the street from the bar," Jerome had said.

From that distance, I couldn't make out his face in detail as I glanced out the storefront window, but the man I saw looked very much like Mr. Fedora. Standing on the other side of the street with a paper in his hands, he was scanning the sidewalk beside him.

"Wait here," I said, determined to confront the man myself. "Follow me," I said to Jerome. "I'm going to have a little chat with him."

Jerome tried to stand in my way. "I wouldn't advise it, Sir," he said, holding up a hand. "That's why you hired me. I'll go and have a little chat with him."

Now, I'm big as far as height and weight goes, but Jerome was really big. Six-five, two-hundred and thirty, give or take a pound. Mostly muscle. His suits were tight across the shoulders and biceps. His shaved head and goatee added a look of professional danger to him.

"Please, Josh," Ella said, her hand on my arm. "He's right. Let him deal with this."

I sat back down on the bar stool and shook my head. "Okay. You're probably right. Go and see what he has to say for himself."

"I can't do anything if he's not threatening you," Jerome said. "But I can deliver a message. I can tell him that you're protected and that he's being watched. If he gets within twenty feet of you, I'll consider it a threat. He won't like the way I deal with a threat."

"What would you do?" Ella asked.

"I'd use my special techniques in persuasion to convince him to leave."

He smiled and then left the bar.

"I wouldn't want to mess with Jerome," Michael offered.

"Me, neither."

While we watched, Jerome walked out of the bar and crossed the street, barely even checking the traffic as he crossed. He made a beeline right to Mr. Fedora, and stopped right in front of the man, who put down his paper. The two men talked, and Jerome gestured to the left and both men glanced down that way. I wondered what Jerome said, but whatever it was, it seemed to have an effect. The man tucked his paper under his arm and walked off to the right. On Jerome's part, he stood and watched, then spoke into a cell.

Finally, he turned around and crossed the street again. It was then I saw a black sedan drive to the right and Jerome stopped and pointed down the street in the direction Mr. Fedora took.

The sedan pulled away and Jerome watched for a moment before coming back inside the bar.

"What happened?" I asked when Jerome arrived back at the bar. He adjusted his jacket and nodded.

"I asked him what he was doing. He said he was just passing time waiting for a friend. I told him that we knew what he was doing and that we were watching him. If he came within 100 feet of you or your properties, he'd have to deal with me. He denied knowing what I was talking about. I pointed down the street and said that there was a security van watching the street and had everything on tape. Then I asked him to be on his way. He complied."

"I saw you speaking with someone in a black sedan," I replied. "Who was that?"

"It was one of my colleagues, Mitch, who is tailing the man. We're going to find out who this sonofabitch is one way or another."

I nodded, glad that they might be able to find out what he was doing. Then, maybe I could put Mr. Fedora out of my mind.

9

ELLA

We closed the deal on the Park Avenue fixer-upper the first week that both Josh and I were back at work.

It was an extremely fast decision, but we both felt the location was perfect and the project would allow us to have our dream apartment. My office and Josh's office would both look out over Central Park, so it was perfect. I couldn't wait to sit down with Michael and his designers and builders to talk about what we wanted done. The prospect of Josh and I going out to choose appliances and furniture and decorations made me extremely happy.

So it was that I had a spring in my step as I walked across the crosswalk to the coffee shop, Blaine, my bodyguard for the day, in tow. My first few weeks back at work were busy as I tried to catch up with the influx of manuscripts that came over the transom during the holidays. One day, towards the end of January, Josh came down to the office and sat in the chair across from my desk.

"What are you doing here? I thought we were going to keep work and pleasure separate," I said, putting on a serious expression, although I was just teasing.

"You're too tempting," Josh said. "Besides, we're going to be married in April. We've been really good, avoiding each other for the past couple of weeks, but now that everyone knows we're engaged, I figured we could come out of the closet." He stood and came around my desk, sitting on the edge beside me. He leaned down and kissed me. "Finally, I don't really care anymore what anyone thinks. We're going to be married and what's mine will be yours, and what's yours will be mine. You'll be a part owner as well as an employee."

"I'll expect a bigger office, if that's the case," I said, folding my arms, my expression serious.

"Shall I fire Sharon and install you in her place?" Josh asked and for a moment, I thought he was being serious, but then I saw the gleam in his eyes.

"Sharon can stay. I want you to get rid of that new manager and install me there instead. His office is much bigger that Sharon's."

We both laughed, because neither of us were serious.

"Seriously," I said. "I'm happy to learn the ropes by working as Sharon's assistant. That's good enough for me for now. I'm not arrogant enough to think I should be put in any position beyond that. For now. Maybe one day, I might like to take over the business and run it, but I'm nowhere near that now. I'm still learning."

Josh nodded. "That's a good attitude to have. Ambitious, but aware of your need to learn and grow. One day, when you feel ready, Dominion Publishing will be yours if you want it. But if you want a bigger office, I could probably justify it because you're going to be my wife. Everyone would understand."

"Never," I said and shook my head. "That would be seen as being selfish and arrogant. I love my office. There's nothing wrong with it and a bigger office wouldn't make me any happier."

"Good," Josh said and leaned down to kiss me again. "Now, I have to go back to work. Do you feel like some Vietnamese spring rolls and pho for supper? I have a coupon," he said and held out a flyer he must have picked up somewhere for 10% off our next order.

"Any excuse for Vietnamese, I always say," I replied. I was already imagining the spicy spring rolls, the noodle soup and the other dishes we always ordered. It had become one of our favorite takeout meals and when we ordered it, I always made sure there was enough left over so I could have it the next day for lunch.

"Good. There's a Knicks game on tonight, and I want to watch. I'll get some beer while I'm out."

"Sounds like the perfect way to pass a cold winter night. You have a meeting at the main office?" I asked, curious why he was going out.

"No, I have a meeting with a lead on a story we're working on for the *Chronicle*. It's cloak and dagger stuff." He wagged his eyebrows.

"Cloak and dagger?" I said, frowning. "Is it political? Economic? Crime?"

He smiled. "Maybe a little of all three."

"Be careful," I said, and stood, slipping my arms around his neck. "I don't like the thought of you meeting with unsavory types for a story that your reporters should be doing. You're the boss. You should be safely ensconced in your big corner desk overlooking the newsroom. Or is that just the way it is in the movies?"

"It's that way in real life, too, but this is something I want to take care of personally."

"You can't tell me about it?" I asked, pouting.

"No can do," Josh said. "But maybe one day, you'll read about it in the papers."

"You don't trust me to keep silent about whatever it is?" I asked, feeling a bit hurt. "I'd never say anything to anyone about it."

"It's not that," Josh said, his tone serious. "It's that I wouldn't want to put you in any danger. There are some stories that have big powerful players involved who use unsavory tactics to keep the story quiet. I don't want you to ever be in danger because of something I told you."

"Josh, what kind of story is this?" I asked, suddenly alarmed. "Does it involve the mafia or something?"

Josh shrugged. "Something like that, and I'm not going to say anything more, okay?"

"Is that why Mr. Fedora has been following us?"

He shook his head. "I don't know. Until I know who he is and who he works for, I can't say. But I want to be safe, just in case. Can you trust me with this?" he said, meeting my eyes, his expression firm.

I nodded, knowing Josh had to keep some things private until he felt he could talk about it to me. Some stories were still in the early stages and he needed to keep quiet about them.

"Okay, I understand."

We kissed again and Josh turned to leave. "I'll be home at around seven with the beer and Korean food, so have the television warmed up so we can watch the pre-game talk before it starts."

"I'll be waiting."

Josh left and I exhaled, worried about whatever story his paper was chasing down that he thought was dangerous enough that he couldn't tell me about it for my own safety. I hoped it wasn't the mafia, whether the Italian or the Russian version. It could even be the Irish mafia for all I knew. Each group had their own territories and areas of dominance. Building, shipping, drugs, prostitution... They tended to leave civilians alone as long as you weren't involved in any of their business dealings, but a civilian could be targeted as a way to pay back someone who messed with them. That much I did know from reading about them.

For his sake, I hoped whatever it was, Josh wasn't in any danger.

· · ·

I met with Sharon later in the afternoon, and together, we went over the latest manuscripts I'd done coverage of for the editorial team. She was happy with my work and so I left the meeting feeling really positive about how things were going on the job side. I was pretty sure that even if Josh wasn't going to be my husband, Sharon would want to keep me on as a paid employee, and that's what mattered to me.

I knew that I could probably slide by on my connection to Josh, but I didn't want to. I wanted to go into publishing before I ever met Josh and so I was prepared to work hard and put in the hours, do the grueling thankless work of being an unpaid assistant for six months to prove myself. When I did get a job, I wanted it to be because of my own hard work and not who my future husband was.

I had pride in my abilities and work ethic. I didn't want people whispering behind my back that I got my job with the publisher because of Josh.

I closed my computer and cleaned off my desk, then took the elevator up to the penthouse, wanting to change into some more comfortable clothes for Josh and my evening watching basketball and eating Korean food. When I got inside the apartment, I went right to the bathroom and had a quick shower, just in case Josh had something else on his mind before we ate, which was often the case. When I was finished, I dressed in something sexy but comfortable and went to the kitchen to get out plates and serving spoons for our meal. Then, as Josh instructed, I turned on the flatscreen and turned to the sports channel that carried the Knicks games and plopped down on the sofa in wait.

While I waited, I listened to the chatter on the sports channel as the announcers talked about the game and the season, half an ear on them and half of my mind focused on my Twitter feed, reading the latest news. It was now seven o'clock and I expected Josh home any time with our food and beer. When another fifteen minutes passed without any Josh, I checked my texts and email to see if he had sent a message about being late, but there was nothing. At seven thirty, I started to get alarmed. He usually was really good at sending me text messages if he was going to be late for our plans, and so I was surprised that he hadn't already.

Finally, at 7:45, after the game had already been on for a quarter of an hour, I got a text from him.

JOSH: Sorry I'm going to be late, but something came up about that thing I was talking about and I had to stay later than I planned. I'm on my way now and will be there in twenty minutes with food and beer in hand.

I smiled to myself and sighed with relief.

ELLA: Okay, the game is on and I'm waiting for you. Hope everything is okay...

JOSH: Everything's fine. Don't worry -- just a delay in the meeting I was going to have, so it screwed up my schedule. I'll be there soon.

ELLA: K.

I leaned back, glad that he was fine and there was nothing dangerous about him being so late.

. . .

J osh finally arrived close to eight thirty, a bag of Vietnamese food in one hand and a six-pack of beer in the other.

"Here I am," he said and placed the beer and food on the kitchen island. "Let the bells right out and the banners fly. Feast your eyes on me."

I laughed at the reference to an old cartoon we'd both seen on television one Saturday morning when we were scanning the channels for something to watch before a game.

We sat together at the coffee table and opened the food, grabbed a beer each and watched the game, which was already in progress.

"Cheers," Josh said and held up his bottle of beer. "Sorry I'm late but I hope the food and of course, the company, will make up for it."

"It does," I said and clinked the neck of my beer against his. "More than makes up for it."

"Good," he said and took a sip. He placed his beer down and had a serious expression on his face. "I got delayed due to a thing, and then my other thing was pushed back as a result."

"You sound busy with things," I replied, smiling at his choice of words. "Don't worry. I won't ask about the thing and the other thing."

"Thank you," he said and dug into his spicy beef stir fry. "Because I won't tell you."

I shrugged. "Luckily, you talk in your sleep, so I'll probably find out anyway," I said with an exaggerated sigh.

"I don't talk in my sleep," he said with a huff. Then he glanced at me. "Do I?"

I laughed. "No, you don't. Don't worry. I was just teasing you since you're determined to be all secretive and mysterious."

"Ella, it's not that I want to be secretive. I want to share everything with you, but this particular story is sensitive, and I don't want to risk it. You'll find out if it comes to anything. For all I know right now, it could be just gossip and disinformation."

"It's okay," I said and squeezed his arm. "I understand. I really do. You won't hear another word from me about the stories you work on at the *Chronicle*, okay?"

He looked in my eyes. "Thanks. I'll tell you everything I can."

"I know," I said and turned back to my food, picking up a spicy spring roll with my chopsticks and dipped it into the sauce.

I hoped Josh wasn't just minimizing the risks he and the paper were taking with the story he was working on. There was nothing I could do about it anyway, so I tried to push it out of my mind.

10

JOSH

I CHECKED MY WATCH AND HOPED I WASN'T MAKING A big mistake.

I met with Reg at his office after my brief stop in Ella's office, planning to go over what news he'd found about Mr. Fedora. Reg's Private Detective Colin had been following Mr. Fedora to find out who the hell he was and why he was tracking us. He'd submitted his first report.

"What have you got for me?" I asked, sitting on the chair across from Reg's desk in the security office.

He flipped open a file and turned a few pages.

"Turns out that his name is Grant McPherson. He's a former cop and worked the fraud squad for a decade before he semi-retired to a life as a private investigator."

"How did you find that out?"

"Face recognition software, the origins of which I won't tell you for your own security."

"That's cool. Who is he?"

"McPherson works for Brentford, Wallace and Conroy, a law firm that deals with Wall Street types, doing investigations of clients and companies the law firm represents or is involved in suing."

The name seemed familiar, so I must have heard about the firm in the news.

"I have nothing to do with Wall Street, other than investments the company has made over the years."

"My guess is that he's been investigating MBC for some company that wants to sue or invest in the *Chronicle*. I can't think of any other reason."

Josh nodded and rubbed his chin thoughtfully. "The invest part I'm not concerned with, but the sue part I am. I'll have to go back through our stories on business fraud over the past few years to see which ones might have led to charges. If he keeps trailing us, I'll have to go speak to Messrs. Brentford, Wallace and Conroy and ask them to explain."

"If your paper or one of MBC's news programs did an exposé on one of their clients, it would be enough to make then look for dirt on MBC that they could use as leverage -- to get us to shut up about them."

"We have the First Amendment on our side, if it comes to a defamation lawsuit," Josh said. "But it could get very expensive defending the paper if it comes to that."

I thanked Reg and asked him to keep track of the man while I tried to figure out what story might have led to the law firm researching me and MBC. Not that I was worried about Mr. Fedora any longer. He wasn't personally a threat to either me or Ella, but if he started to harass us, I'd go to the company and demand they explain and call off their dog.

My next task was more research on the story about Ella's father and Henry Garner. MBC had done many investigative reports of a political and economic nature over the years. My father had been particularly interested in financial fraud. He was an idealist, who believed that it was wrong for the rich and powerful to hide their money from the IRS, even if there were legitimate offshore investments that could be made to keep it from taxation.

My father was even more adamant about politicians who used their insider knowledge of economic conditions to profit by buying or selling stocks based on upcoming deals or stock performance or company intelligence. That had been the case with Garner and the whole business from before he was governor. Garner learned about an upcoming financial report of a company under federal investigation for fraud and had sold his stock, taking a big profit the day before the news was made public and the stock price fell precipitously.

That was against the law, and as a result, Garner was charged and convicted. He'd had a couple other previous charges against him for financial fraud that had never resulted in anything but fines, but finally, he must have reached the threshold for fraud with a judge and he got time.

What aroused suspicion on my part had been the fact that Carlson hadn't been charged. I figured he'd either been a witness for the government's financial crimes unit or had got away with his involvement for some reason. I feared it might have been because of a bribe he'd paid. One of the contacts

I'd discussed the case with had said he'd always been suspicious about why Carlson hadn't been charged along with Garner.

I'd arranged to meet with Tim Mathis, a veteran in the news world and one of my father's former reporters who worked on the case years earlier. Tim agreed to meet with me at a bar in the financial district, and I'd taken Reg with me when I went, just to be on the safe side. While I went inside, Reg stayed on the sidewalk outside the bar and watched the area in case we'd been followed. While I wasn't worried about any threat from Mr. Fedora, aka Grant McPherson, any longer, I was interested in whether he kept following me.

The bar wasn't too packed when Reg and I arrived, with the happy hour crowd limited and so I joined Tim Mathis, a grey-haired man wearing half-eye glasses, sitting at a table by the storefront, reading a copy of the New York Times and drinking a beer.

"Tim Mathis?" I asked and waited for his response.

"That's me," he replied. He glanced up at me and then at Reg, who nodded and went to sit at a nearby table.

I extended my hand to Mathis and we shook, then I sat on the chair across from him while he folded up his paper.

"Sorry to hear about your father," Tim said after I had given my order of a beer to the waitress.

"Thanks," I said. "It was fast. We were all shocked even though we knew he was dying."

"He was a great man," Tim said softly. "Self-made, totally committed to journalism. He will be missed."

"He will be," I replied. "Thanks for your card and flowers."

"Don't mention it. I hear you're the big cheese now at the *Chronicle*," Tim said, a good-natured ribbing in his tone. "I was just reading your competition."

I nodded. "We're hoping to resurrect it. It has a great history."

"That it does."

Preliminaries out of the way, I decided to dive right in.

"So, I wanted to talk with you about the story you did for MBC on Henry Garner, Emmet Carlson's partner, who was convicted of insider trading back in the nineties."

Mathis went over the story for a few moments, recalling how they were given some leads to track down about a stock deal that had been suspiciously close to the day news was released about the company being charged with fraud and it turned up Garner. They'd followed Garner for several months before they'd been able to write anything substantive. When Garner was finally charged, it was a big local scandal in New Hampshire and notable to people who followed Wall Street, but to people outside of the financial world, it would be nothing much of interest. Just another inside trader who was caught. The only difference was that this time, he went to prison.

Usually, these kinds of crimes led to fines and nothing more. Garner was a repeat offender, so he finally got a sentence of time in a comfy white-collar prison, where he'd spent a decade.

End of story.

Emmet Carlson was somehow spared being charged, despite the fact that the two ran the small investment firm together. I figured that Carlson had nothing to do with that stock or sale. But usually, with a small firm like that, the partners would be involved in any decision to buy or sell stock.

"Why wasn't Carlson charged?" I asked point blank.

Mathis shrugged. "Your guess is as good as mine. Apparently, Security and Exchange Commission prosecutors decided he had nothing to with that sale and didn't charge him. He didn't even testify at the trial. I imagine he was questioned by their investigators but wasn't charged nor did he testify against Garner. There is footage of him speaking with the press about the fines Garner paid, and the charges. He defended Garner and said it was a misunderstanding."

"Funny that he defended him, when it was clearly breaking the law."

"Well, he may have cooperated with the SEC. Or he may have been innocent. Either way, it's old news. Why are you looking into it now? Carlson's respected as the Governor of New Hampshire. He's been clean from what I can see for two decades and Garner's dead, so..."

"I'm engaged to Ella Carlson, his daughter."

"Congratulations," Mathis said and held up his beer bottle in a toast. "I can see why you might want to bone up on the case."

I nodded. "I just wanted to know about the case and MBC's role in it so I can get along with my future father-in-law. He's not too well-disposed towards MBC because of our station's exposé on Garner, shall we say."

"Politicians always hate the press," Mathis said with a laugh and took a long sip of his beer. "They love us when we make them look good, but when we don't, they condemn us."

"Isn't that the truth?" I replied and did the same.

We talked a few minutes longer about his role in the program on Garner and then I shook his hand once more and left the bar. While it had been good to speak with Mathis, he really didn't give me much more information than I already had gleaned from reading the reports of the day and watching MBC's program on the story. We drove back to the building and after I parked the vehicle, Reg and I went up to the main floor security office to go over the plans to call off the protection we'd had on Ella and me for the last while.

Now that I knew who Mr. Fedora was, I wasn't as concerned about some nutcase following us around with plans of vengeance. He was just a PI looking for some information on me for his client.

It was a relief not to worry about personal security for us.

I went up to the penthouse and Ella was already there, dressed in her bathrobe, her hair wet.

"What's up?" I asked when I took her into my arms. "You just had a shower?"

"I did," she replied and kissed me. "I went for a bike ride and got all sweaty."

"All sweaty, hmm?" I asked and nuzzled her neck. She smelled so good, and her skin was warm and soft against my lips. She closed her eyes and sighed as I opened her robe and kissed her throat.

"You're going to make me all sweaty again if you keep that up."

I smiled and moved lower.

"That's my plan."

And then, for the next half hour at least, I forgot all about Governor Carlson, his business partner Henry Garner and my meeting with Mathis, losing myself in Ella's delicious body.

Later, after a meal of leftovers from the night before, Ella and I snuggled together on the sofa and watched the news.

"We can call off the dogs," I said and turned to her.

"What do you mean?"

I told her about Mr. Fedora and who he really was.

"Oh, thank God," she said and exhaled. "That means we don't have to worry it's some stalker who wants to hurt either of us, right?"

"Right," I said and pulled her closer. "Whoever hired the law firm to hire him to get info on me might want to harm me or MBC financially, but not likely physically. We can stop the personal security detail."

"Good," Ella said. "The guys are great, don't get me wrong, but I want to be able to go out and just wander sometimes.

When you have someone following you, it's hard to feel free."

"Well, now you are free to roam, if you so desire."

She smiled and snuggled into my arms and that was the way we passed the evening.

11

ELLA

I WAS SO GLAD TO BE FREE OF OUR SECURITY DETAIL that I went out the next day and just walked along the East River, enjoying the sights. It felt good to be finally free of the worry that Mr. Fedora would show up and shoot one or the other of us over some slight he perceived Josh, or his company had done years ago. I bought a coffee and worked through one of my breaks so I could take some time off at the end of the day and then I sat on a bench along the pathway bordering the East River and just enjoyed myself.

I imagined how the next couple of months would go as Josh and I worked to get the apartment in order for our move-in date, how we'd be pressed to get the wedding all arranged by Easter, and how I'd manage my workload so we could take some time off and go somewhere to be completely by ourselves for a week. It was nice to have those kinds of things to occupy my mind. My past life in New Hampshire seemed so far away at that moment that I could scarcely believe less than a year earlier, I was depressed and feeling like my life was over.

Now, everything was good. I couldn't look at anything in my life and wish it was different. I often felt like pinching myself and seeing if this was some sort of dream or hallucination, but it wasn't. It was really happening.

I'd met my own Mr. Big, and I was having my own story of happy ever after.

My cell dinged, signaling an incoming text.

It was Steph.

We hadn't been in contact for more than a week and I felt a bit bad that I'd neglected her. I vaguely remembered she'd decided to apply to Oxford for her Masters, after it looked like she would graduate with one of the highest GPAs in her graduating class. I had hoped she would come to live in Manhattan, but she wanted to do her MA instead.

STEPH: Hey, girlfriend. What's up? I miss you.

ELLA: I'm fantastic. How are you? How was your Christmas? How are classes going? You decided to take one more semester of classes for your honors, right?

STEPH: That's right. I'll graduate in the spring. Then, this girl is going to Europe for a backpacking trip with big sis.

ELLA: That sounds wonderful. You need a break, working so hard like you have. What about Oxford? You should be hearing back soon, right?

STEPH: My advisor thinks I'm a shoo-in because of my grades and great recommendations plus my extra-curricular activities. I'll be hearing back within a week.

ELLA: That would be so terrific for you. Fingers crossed.

STEPH: *Thanks. The semester starts in October, so I'd be going for a year of courses and then the thesis work.*

ELLA: *Will you come to Manhattan at that point?*

STEPH: *We'll see. It's my fallback plan. If I don't get in, I'll go backpacking with Char and then move to Manhattan and bug you.*

ELLA: *You could never bug me.*

Steph's younger sister Charlene was working in the restaurant business, waiting tables while she took courses and would be finished in the Spring as well.

STEPH: *What's up with you and Mr. Handsome?*

ELLA: *We set the date.*

STEPH: SHUT THE FRONT DOOR! *When?*

ELLA: *Easter Saturday.*

STEPH: *Wow - that's so soon. What's the rush? Will you even be able to get everything ready by then? You'll have to book a church and a venue...*

ELLA: *Josh wanted to get married right away. I said we should wait three months at least. We're going to have the ceremony in LA at David's mansion so it's no problem booking a venue or anything. Of course, I want you to be my maid of honor.*

STEPH: *LA? That sounds great. Please don't make me wear a silly dress. That's all I ask. Something tasteful, okay?*

ELLA: *I'll let you pick out your dress. How's that?*

STEPH: *Perfect. I'll try to coordinate with you, but you know me. I have this giraffe physique and not every style looks good on me.*

ELLA: *More like a gazelle physique. Don't put yourself down like that.*

STEPH: *I happen to love giraffes, kiddo. ;)*

ELLA: *LOL*

STEPH: *Who will be best man?*

ELLA: *I don't know who he'll ask. Probably David, I would think.*

STEPH: *OMG, David McIntyre. I'm in love already. He's such a hunk of dangerous man-flesh. Will the other brothers be there? Is there one who I could snag?*

ELLA: *I thought you were going to Oxford in October...*

STEPH: *I might reconsider if I could snag him. Seriously, Ella. David is a babe.*

ELLA: *He's actually quite sweet once you get to know him.*

STEPH: *That's right -- you and Josh spent time in LA at Christmas. We haven't talked for almost two weeks. Spill, sister. What's he really like? He has such a bad-boy persona.*

ELLA: *David's quite deep, when you get to know him. He seems really rough around the edges when he performs but he was a perfect gentleman the whole time we were there. Of course, he just lost Terry, one of his band members and I think it hit him really hard.*

STEPH: Yeah, it must have been traumatic. I heard that they finished the latest EP and will be going on tour with the new guy.

ELLA: Yes. David seems to have recovered, but Josh says there's a sadness in him that wasn't there before. He wants us to spend the honeymoon there, too, but maybe we'll go somewhere exotic for a week. Bora Bora or French Polynesia.

STEPH: You should. You deserve it, kiddo. What do your parents think of Josh? Is your dad okay with it? I know there was that thing with the business partner back in the day.

ELLA: Mom gave him the word and he was a gentleman the entire two days we were at their place.

STEPH: That's good. The last thing you two need is a family feud to get between you.

ELLA: I know. I'm glad they put down the muskets and agreed to a truce.

STEPH: How's your writing going? Have you finished your own book yet?

ELLA: Still writing it. Maybe one of these days...

STEPH: You're too busy living your own Mr. Big fantasy to write about it, I guess. Now, we have to find one for me.

ELLA: Maybe in Oxford? Some brainy hunk with glasses and tattoos, spouting philosophy?

STEPH: I wish. Oh, you'll never guess who I ran into at the chiropractor last week. None other than Jerkface himself.

ELLA: UGH! That must have been awkward.

STEPH: *Oh, yeah. We both had to sit in the waiting room for at least fifteen mins. He tried to make small talk. Said he'd heard you had a new BF. I really rubbed it in, saying that he was very rich and very smart.*

ELLA: *What did Jerkface say? I hope he was green with envy.*

STEPH: *Man, I could almost see the steam coming out of his ears, but he played it so cool like it was nothing to him. I knew better. You are so lucky you got rid of him, Ellie. I'm serious. He may be a hunk but IMO he's a hunk of sh*t.*

ELLA: *My words exactly. Welp, I gotta go. Get back to the office and finish reading my latest batch of manuscripts.*

STEPH: *Later, kiddo. Big smoochies.*

ELLA: *Big smoochies back at ya! XOXOXO*

STEPH: *XOXOXO*

I smiled to myself as I read over the exchange.

I missed my girl Steph, but if she got accepted to Oxford for her MA, she'd be gone for the next couple of years and we wouldn't see each other except on holidays. We'd been friends forever so I wasn't worried that we'd grow apart, but I would miss her. She'd be part of my wedding and so she'd be part of my life for the rest of it -- I hoped.

As for her finding someone, Steph was one of those bold women who asked men out on dates. I didn't worry about her being alone. She'd find someone when she was good and ready. She was very ambitious and had a list of things to accomplish before she was willing to find a partner and settle down. Oxford was first on the list and after that, a PhD.

She had a heavyweight mind and was intimidating despite the fact she was a total geek girl. She'd have to find a very special man to make her happy. One who was tall enough to at least look her in the eyes.

W e met with Josh's brother Michael, his architect and interior designer the following week to decide what to do with our apartment. The architect went over options for redesigning the living room / dining room / kitchen. Josh wanted one big room so that we could see each other when we were cooking, watching television or having dinner. He grew up in a house with a formal dining room that was separate from the kitchen and he liked the idea of a great room. I kind of preferred the more traditional separation of the rooms, but it seemed really important to Josh, so I said sure -- as long as there was one formal dining room for big family dinners, I was okay with it. Besides, there would be more than enough room in the penthouse apartment for a separate dining room. There would be an office for Josh, one for me, and our master suite. Plus, one guest bedroom that would serve as a nursery when we decided to have a baby.

We both wanted the apartment to be filled with light, and so all the windows would be replaced and enlarged where possible. The flooring would be a mix of blond hardwoods, pale grey ceramic tile and light grey carpet. We decided on a French provincial style for the cabinets in the kitchen and selected the fixtures and appliances to fit. Josh insisted on a chef's kitchen and I didn't argue. I could see us cooking together and hosting dinner parties with our family and friends.

What I was really interested in was my own office, and of course, the patio on the rooftop.

As for my office, it was the smaller of the two, but I didn't want or need anything bigger. There would be a built-in desk and shelving unit, with a hutch where I could store my supplies. There would even be room for a recliner so I could sit and read if I wanted to. It would be my office away from the office.

"When we have kids, you could work from home if you wanted," Josh said while we looked over the room's layout.

"That would be optimal," I said.

We also checked out the plans for the rooftop space. It would be amazing to be able to see the park and city. The view would be breathtaking. I could imagine Josh and I up there cooking on a big grill, sitting on a nice sectional patio set, or sitting in our own hot tub, watching the clouds float by. The rooftop space was big enough that we could even have a space set aside for a container garden and I could grow fresh vegetables.

When we saw the space, it was the first week in January and the weather was cold and blustery, but I could see the space in my head during the spring, summer and fall. If we built an enclosed space, and had some lattice put up to moderate the wind, it would be really pleasant. There was a small area where we could even put a swing set and sand-box, when we had children.

I watched Josh looking over the plans, his face bright with excitement, as he spoke with the architect and designer about possible layouts for the space. He turned to me, smiling, his blue eyes so warm, and I could sense his happiness. He leaned over when he caught my eye and kissed me.

"You like?" he asked, holding up one of the drawings.

"I can't wait to see it when it's done."

"Me, either. We're so lucky we found this place. It's going to be perfect."

It was going to be perfect -- just like our life together.

12

JOSH

THE FOLLOWING WEEK WENT FAST, AND THE ONLY ITEM on my agenda to accomplish in preparation for the wedding was a call to David to confirm everything. I selected his number for a Skype and waited, smiling at the prospect of how he'd react to the plans.

Finally, he answered and there he was, but he didn't seem quite as chipper as I expected. In fact, he seemed downright depressed.

"Hey," I said when he sounded down. "What's the matter? I called to ask if we could have the wedding at your place on Easter Saturday."

"Oh, man, of course you can," he said, his face lighting up finally. "I'm just in that post-production blues period after a project is finished and you wait for critical reception. You know, you send the EP out to critics and hope for the best. I'm just impatient, I guess and worried that people won't like it."

"People will love it," I said, remembering the music I heard when I was there earlier in the year. "You guys have a huge fan base and they always love your work."

"I hope so, but with Terry gone, I'm sure people will make a fuss. We dedicated the EP to him so I hope that his fans will be happy. So, Easter Saturday, huh? I can't wait. We'll invite all the brothers, and of course, Ella's family and friends. It'll be great."

"Good," I said, relaxing a little. "Both Ella and I thought it would be a great location. We'll probably fly to some exotic all-inclusive place for our honeymoon, but we wanted to come there for a few days before the wedding and spend time there."

"I'm marking my calendar now. I'll call my chef guy and have him do the catering. I have a decorating guy, too. He'll do the flowers and shit like that. If you guys want, you should fly down for a weekend and we can iron it all out. In fact, why don't we make a plan now? When can you two get away and come out here?"

"I'll talk to Ella and get back to you."

"Good," David said. "This will keep my mind busy. You know I love any chance to have people here. Are you calling the brothers or should I?"

"No, that's okay. I'll call them and ask them to be there."

"Great," he said, and I was happy that he seemed so genuinely pleased about hosting the wedding. We talked a few moments longer about nothing in particular and then said goodbye. I hung up and checked the time. I had an early meeting that day and hadn't got my bike ride in, so I decided to take time mid-afternoon to go for a ride. The weather was good, and it was still sunny, and the streets were pretty clear of snow, so it was perfect timing.

I changed into my riding clothes and grabbed my bike, taking it downstairs. When I got to the street and climbed onto it, I adjusted my helmet and it was then I saw Mr. Fedora across the street once more. I exhaled in anger and decided to confront the man myself.

I rode across the street at the crosswalk and stopped in front of him, still on the bike. He glanced up from his paper and I caught a smile on his face.

"I know who you are and who you're working for," I said, unable to keep anger out of my voice.

"But you don't know why," he replied, grinning.

"I would if you told me."

He glanced left and right, and then stepped closer. "You should ask Ms. Conroy."

Then he folded his paper and walked away.

I followed him, riding beside him on my bike. "Who the hell is Ms. Conroy?"

"You don't remember the names of your sex partners? Alicia Conroy, twenty-four, daughter of James Conroy. Of Brentford, Wallace and Conroy?"

Then the name did ring a bell and I had an image of a blonde young woman with big tits who had charmed the pants off me months ago after a drunken night in a bar. It was the month before I met Ella.

Crap...

There could be only one reason her father, a partner with the law firm who hired McPherson, was interested in me.

"Don't tell me," I said and held up a hand. "She's--."

"She's pregnant. And she's pretty sure you're her baby-daddy." McPherson smiled widely.

"We had sex twice," I said, a sense of dread filling me. "She told me she was on the pill. I used a condom for protection -- both times. There's no way she's pregnant with my child."

"You sure about that?"

"I'm pretty sure I tested the condoms after and they were intact, so I don't know how she could get pregnant."

"She said you were both really drunk and that there might have been contact before you put on the condom."

I tried to remember that night, but it was pretty fuzzy, and we were both quite drunk. I do remember us being naked and rolling around in the bed before we fucked. There was a lot of oral play before and then we got down to business. I did use a condom. Both times.

"I used a condom."

"Regardless of what you think, she is pregnant and she says you're the only man she slept with during that cycle, so it's either the immaculate conception or somehow your jizz got inside of her before you put the condom on. My client wants you to do a paternity test."

"Fine," I said and shrugged. "You could have asked me. I'd be happy to comply, because I know I'm not the father. Why didn't you just ask weeks ago when I first saw you hanging around my office building?"

"My client wanted to know what kind of man you were just in case you are the father of his daughter's child."

I sighed. "Look, I'm one hundred percent certain that I'm not the father. I'll do the paternity test -- whatever you need. Tell me where to go and what to do. I'm engaged to be married and I want this cleared up as soon as possible."

"Good," McPherson said and reached into his jacket pocket. "Here's the court order for a test. This will prove one way or the other if you're the father." He handed me an envelope containing what I expected was a court order for a paternity test.

I took it from him. "You know, this whole business could have been settled a month ago if you'd just asked for a meeting and told me about this."

"My client wasn't sure you were the father. Seems that Alicia didn't want to name you at first, so my client did some research on the men she dated in the months surrounding the date she became pregnant. You're one of three men who are possible fathers. He convinced her to petition to have you tested."

"Have the other men taken tests?"

"Yes. Both came back negative. It looks like you're the one."

I shook my head, certain that there was no way it was me. "I guess the test will prove otherwise, so there must have been someone else."

Then, I tucked the envelope into my jacket interior pocket and drove off.

I needed a very long ride around the river to work off the anger I felt at this most recent turn of events...

W hen I arrived back at the building, I went right up to the apartment and had a shower. In the shower, I went over what I could remember about my encounter with Alicia Conroy. We met at a local club when I was out with Keith on a nice summer night earlier in the year. We'd done shots as a group, we danced, and somehow, Alicia and I paired off and one thing led to another. We left together and took a cab back to the apartment, where we had a very tipsy encounter and then a much more sober encounter if somewhat hung over, the next morning. Alicia was vivacious and pretty with luscious curves and blonde hair down to her waist.

She was impressed with my name and family connections, and indicated she'd be interested in seeing me again. I said sure, give me your number, but I never did call her for a repeat performance. While enjoyable sexually, she just didn't strike me as girlfriend material.

I was certain that I'd used a condom both times we had sex. Drunk or sober, I always used protection for my sake more than anything. I didn't want to get a disease or someone pregnant.

That was the last thing on my mind.

I finished showering and got dressed, standing in the mirror, fastening my tie. It was then I remembered the first time we fucked. She'd got on top of me before I could put on a condom and had tried to ride me, but I stopped her.

"Whoa, girl," I had said and lifted her off me. "Wait a minute..." I'd reached into the drawer of my bedside table and pulled out a condom, fumbling in my drunken way with the condom, rolling it over my erection.

Then, we'd fucked. I removed the condom afterwards and tied it off. No leaks. There had been none the second time, either.

"If you got her pregnant, you're a dumb fuck," I said to myself.

I went to my office and checked my email. Then I called George, my lawyer who handled personal matters.

"Hey, George, I was served with a petition to undergo a paternity test for a woman I had sex with last summer. She's pregnant and claims I'm the only one who could be the father."

I heard George exhale on the other end of the line.

"You have to comply and go to the lab, get tested. If it comes back that you're the likely father, you'll have to provide child support."

I took in a deep breath. "Look, George, I used a condom both times we had sex, and I checked both times and the condom was intact. There's no way that it's my kid."

"Was there any unprotected genital-to-genital contact?"

I made a face. "There was a very brief amount of contact when she was eager to get going but I stopped her before there was any real penetration. Could she get pregnant from what tiny amount of material might have been present?"

"Absolutely. It happens. It's very rare and highly unlikely, especially if she was also on the pill. But it has happened before. You better be prepared."

I rubbed my forehead, angry with myself that I'd been drinking too hard and been too promiscuous after Christie and I broke up. I had tried to drown my sorrows in pussy and probably had gotten myself into big trouble.

"Thanks. I'll let you know what happens. How much will I be on the hook for, if it is my child?"

"You're very rich. The judge will expect you to raise this child in a manner in keeping with your current lifestyle. As a multi-millionaire with a large income, it will be a lot."

"Okay, thanks. Figure something out for me, just in case."

"I will. Sorry about this, Josh, but it's the law."

"I know," I said and ended the call, feeling an urge to smash something.

I sat in the silence of my office for a few moments, trying to calm myself. I knew what I had to do. I had to go right down and tell Ella. I'd made a promise to be totally honest with her about everything.

I wasn't going to break that promise now, even if I was pretty sure the whole business would amount to nothing.

I took the elevator down to her floor and after saying hello to the receptionist, I went back to Ella's office. She had her head buried in a manuscript and glanced up almost in a daze when I knocked on the open door.

"Can I come in?" I asked and entered the office, my hand on the doorknob. "We need to talk. In private."

"Sure," she said and blinked, pushing the manuscript away. "Come in. Close the door."

I closed it and went over to her, kissing her and stroking her cheek.

"What's the matter?" she asked, her eyes wide. "Is it bad news? You look grim."

I leaned on the desk beside her and took her hand. "I have something to tell you. It's going to be upsetting."

"Josh, you're scaring me."

"I don't mean to, but something happened." I hesitated, not knowing how to phrase it. I decided to just come out and say it point blank. "A woman I had sex with in the summer before we met has petitioned to force me to do a paternity test."

Her mouth dropped open and she glanced away, not saying anything.

Finally, she looked back into my eyes. "Is this possible? Do you think you might be the father?"

I shook my head. "I used a condom both times we had sex, but there was a moment when she kind of got on top of me before I put one on. There was maybe," I said and held out my finger and thumb an inch apart, "maybe a small bit of penetration before. I stopped her and put on the condom, but my lawyer tells me that there is a very small chance I am the father if so."

"Oh, Josh, I'm so sorry..."

I exhaled. "Me, too."

Ella stood and slipped her arms around my neck, leaning against me, her face beside mine. We kissed warmly and then she pulled back.

"Whatever happens, I'm with you. If it's your child, you have to do what's right."

"Thank you," I said, feeling relieved she was being so supportive right away. "I was afraid you'd be really mad."

"How could I be mad? I've been reckless before and could have become pregnant. I was just lucky a couple of times when, you know, Jerkface and I had unprotected sex. So, who am I to judge?"

"You and Derek had unprotected sex?"

She widened her eyes. "A couple of times when we both drank too much, yes. But don't worry. I've been tested for STDs and I'm clean."

"I didn't even think of that," I said. "Thank you for being so understanding."

She kissed me and ran her hand through my hair. "Whatever happens, we're in this together, right?"

"We are," I said.

"As long as you don't replace me with her, I don't care."

"Never," I said and pulled her more tightly against me.

I held her in my arms and hoped that the test would be negative. I couldn't wait to get it done and put it all behind us.

13

ELLA

When Josh left my office, I closed the door and the encouraging smile I had plastered on my face fell. I sat down at my desk and had a quick cry.

It was completely silly of me to cry about it. Josh had several sexual partners between his breakup with Christie and meeting me. There was nothing wrong with it. He had always been very careful when we made love to use a condom, not wanting to take a risk and I appreciated that. I realized that if he did get the woman pregnant, it had been a total accident, and not due to him being an uncaring lout.

Still, it would mean he had a child in the world with another woman -- a child he would look after and be responsible for. That child, and not one of ours, would be his first-born. It was silly of me, but my perfect little world got a small dent in it.

I felt totally small and petty, but I also felt this profound sense of sadness. I wanted him to be my only husband and I his only wife. I wanted our family to be his only family. If the baby was his, that would mean he always had another family, even if he didn't love the child's mother. Then I kicked myself. I shouldn't be thinking that way. I should be thinking that if this baby was his, it was his baby. His *child*. It was a product of him, and I loved him more than anything.

I would love his child, even if it wasn't mine.

I wiped my eyes and picked up the manuscript I was currently reading and tried to continue. The whole business was completely out of my hands and so there was nothing I could do but support Josh in whatever happened.

That's what a good fiancée would do. If I was going to be his fiancée, I would be the very best kind possible.

For the next hour before the end of the day, I tried to keep my mind off the issue and focus on my work. When five thirty rolled around, I shut off my computer and cleaned off my desk, putting my files away. I popped my head into Sharon's office and said goodnight, checking if our breakfast meeting was on, and then I went up to the penthouse.

Josh was still working, so I went into the kitchen and checked out the refrigerator to see what we might have for supper. There was frozen chicken in the freezer, and some limp looking carrots in the bottom of the crisper. But there was a lemon, and I had lots of garlic and olive oil and a container of oregano in the spice drawer. I could make Greek Chicken with rice pilaf.

So I did. Cooking helped take my mind off the situation, and with some music playing in the background, I was able to spend the next hour preparing the meal, then cooking it. By the time Josh arrived, the chicken was finishing in the oven, the rice pilaf was steaming away on the stove and I had a cold bottle of beer ready for him. Mine was already half empty.

"Here," I said and handed him his bottle. "You need this after the day you've had."

"You got that right," he said.

I held my bottle up for a toast. He exhaled and we clinked bottles together. Then, he took a long sip before sitting at the island. I went to him and he pulled me into his arms, kissing me before taking another sip.

"I smell something delicious," he said and glanced at the kitchen. "What's cooking? It smells Mediterranean."

"Greek Chicken stuffed with feta in a lemon garlic sauce. Rice pilaf. Roasted carrots."

"Mmm," he said and closed his eyes. "Sounds delicious. I'm glad it's your night to manage supper. I'm exhausted and just want to crash on the sofa and watch something mindless."

"That sounds exactly like I feel, so you're on."

While I finished the chicken, adding some butter and wine to make the sauce, Josh set the table and we sat down for our meal. Outside, the sun had set, and the lights of the city were visible for miles. It was a great view.

"I'll miss this great vista when we move into our new place, but we still have a pretty sweet view."

"It's going to be fantastic," Josh said and we had another toast. "To our new life together."

"To our new life. Together, we can manage anything that comes our way."

After we finished our meal and cleaned up, we went to the living room and snuggled on the sofa. Josh took over the remote and flipped through channels, looking for something interesting to watch. In the end, he settled on a game, with sound turned down low. He pulled me closer, his arm around my shoulder, and put his feet up on the coffee table.

"So, tell me how you're doing," he said, his voice soft.

"I'm fine," I said and laid my head against his shoulder.

He turned and caught my eye, his expression serious. "Tell me the truth. How are you feeling about it? You must be upset."

I gave him a weak smile. "I won't lie and say it didn't upset me, but more for you than out of jealousy."

He nodded, but then I kicked myself. "No, let me correct that. I am jealous. If this is your baby, it will be your first child, not the ones you have with me."

"I'm so sorry about this," Josh said and shook his head. "I've always been so careful about it, because my father drummed it into us as young men that we had to be responsible. But that night, I was a little too drunk."

"I'll deal with it, Josh," I said. "I'm all grown up and will support you, no matter what the outcome."

"Thanks," he said and kissed me tenderly. "Hopefully, it's not mine and we can move on and put all of this behind us. If it is mine, we'll do our best to deal with it. I won't deny my responsibility if it is my child. But she won't ever get in between us, Ella. I promise that She meant nothing to me but a nice fuck when I was hurting after Christie. That's it. If this child is mine, I will be a good parent and make sure I provide for it, and get to know him or her, but it will never interfere with us or our family."

"I know," I said and smiled. "You're a good man, Josh. I know you'll do the right thing."

He was. When he did the right thing, I'd be right there with him.

He got the call from the lab one day during lunch, when we had come up to the apartment to eat together and go over some plans for the apartment. The receptionist had a date for Josh to go for the paternity test. I'd almost forgotten about it, but the question remained this little sense of gloom in my otherwise happy life. We'd been busy looking at kitchen appliances, picking ones out for our apartment when he got the call.

He answered his cell and spoke with the person on the other end of the line. "Oh, yeah," he said and ran his fingers through his hair, which was getting way too long. He jumped up and opened his laptop, checking his calendar to make sure he could make the date, and then put down his cell. "Yes, I can make it. Thanks."

He ended the call and stood looking at me.

"That was the lab," I said.

"Yep. I'm going down on Tuesday afternoon for the test."

"How long will it take?"

"Two days. I guess we'll know by the end of next week, one way or the other."

I sighed. "Then we can move on."

"Yes," he said and pulled on his jacket. "Then we can move on. I have a meeting in fifteen, so I'm heading back downstairs."

"Me, too," I said. "Back to the slush pile."

I grabbed my bag and the two of us went to the elevator, and then down to our respective floors. Josh kissed me before he got off the elevator.

"Tonight, we should go out for supper. I feel like meatballs."

I smiled. "Meatballs are always good."

Then, he was gone, and I exhaled and tried to clear my mind for the rest of the afternoon. Next week couldn't come fast enough.

S haron wanted me to start sitting in on the editorial meetings, so I could get a sense of the kind of dilemmas an editor faced. It meant I was moving up in the world and was exciting. Editors did more than just edit manuscripts. They decided on what books to buy and what books to promote and had to pitch them to the management team. I would start as an assistant editor as soon as my six month-unpaid internship finished, which would coincide with my return from our honeymoon.

The next couple of months would be me learning my new job. So far, I'd spent my time reading manuscripts that were sent to us from various agents who the company did business with on a regular basis. I also got the manuscripts that came in without an agent. They were unsolicited manuscripts. While we usually didn't buy any of those, we had to read them just in case there was a gem that we didn't want to miss. There were horror stories of manuscripts that had been rejected without being read that went on to make the publisher who did buy the book millions.

It was rare for that to happen, but Dominion Publishing, an imprint of Macintyre Publishing, didn't want to be the one who let a bestseller get away.

I'd met all the usual editors during my work at Dominion, but we had some new staff and it was my first real time sitting in an editorial meeting where actual decisions would be made. I wasn't expected to speak or present anything -- just soak up the ambience and learn the ropes.

I couldn't wait.

A t three o'clock, I sat with my laptop at the back of the room, behind Sharon, and listened to the editors talk. There was some good-natured banter among the editors for the first ten minutes as they discussed the latest news in the publishing world -- what books had been a hit or miss at other publishing houses and what authors had signed big deals and what agents were hot at the moment with their fingers on the pulse of the readership.

It was all so exciting to me, because I tended to read the rejects and books that no one would want. Seeing the editors discuss big name authors with million-dollar deals made me envious and I dreamed of the day when I, too, might sign such a deal or find a book worth a million-dollar deal.

That dream was a long way off. I hadn't even finished my chick lit book yet, stuck as I was on the second plot point, so even the idea of finishing a novel was a big deal for me. I knew it would take years before I ever signed a deal, if then. But it was inspirational, listening to them discuss this or that author, this or that deal.

When the meeting was over, Krista, one of the young editorial assistants caught up with me in the hallway. In her early thirties, she was tall and gangly, reminding me of Steph a bit in her physical appearance. She wore funky dark-rimmed cat's eye glasses and had her hair back in a perky ponytail. You could have put a pink sweater on her and handed her pom poms and she'd be a perfect cheerleader type.

"So, how did you like your first real editorial meeting?"

"It was great," I said, giving her a big smile. "So exciting to sit in on an editorial meeting."

"How long have you been with Dominion again?" she asked, frowning. "Three months?"

"Four," I replied. "How about you?"

"Three years," Krista said, her eyebrows raised. "It took me three years to move from being a lowly admin assistant to Maria, the acquisitions editor, to an editorial assistant and I have an MA in English. I heard you're starting as an editorial assistant with Sharon when your internship is over. Talk about lucky."

I glanced at her because her tone sounded anything but happy for me. It sounded pissed.

I smiled, not wanting to get into a pissing match with her. "I'm really excited."

"Of course, you're also marrying the big boss, so..." Krista said, when we stopped outside my office door.

"I am," I said and didn't say anything else on the subject. "Nice to talk with you."

I went inside my office and closed the door in her face, my blood pressure up about twenty points. I stood with my back to the door for a moment and took in a deep breath, trying to calm myself.

Krista had a lot of nerve...

Of course, even I had to admit that I was getting a plum job in Dominion Publishing after only six months on the job as an intern. Was it because Sharon was going along with Josh or was it because she felt I deserved it?

I wanted the job, but I honestly didn't feel I deserved it just because I was marrying Josh...

Was it totally unfair that I was getting a paid job as an editorial assistant?

I went around and sat behind my desk, suddenly unsettled about everything. The very last thing I wanted was to get a job which I wasn't qualified to do or entitled to do. Yes, I had an undergraduate degree in English, and yes, I had worked as an editor for the school literary magazine. During my time at Dominion, I'd picked a few good manuscripts that the company ultimately bought. I had even succeeded in picking out three manuscripts that had been slipped into the slush pile as a test of my judgement.

But I had only worked as a slush reader for the past four months.

Did they promote all their interns after so short a time with equal qualifications?

Or was it nepotism?

With that question unsettled, I spent the rest of the afternoon trying to focus, but it was hard, and my mind kept coming back to Krista's expression and tone.

14

JOSH

THE BIGGEST PROBLEM FACING ME THAT DAY WAS staying focused. With everything going on in my personal life -- the engagement and upcoming wedding, renovating the new apartment, and the paternity issue -- my mind kept wandering away from the matter at hand. Which, at that precise moment, was a financial forecast for the rest of the year. Not my favorite part of being CEO of MBC but one of the most important. I had to keep on top of the numbers and make sure the financials were solid. I trusted my finance team utterly so when they told me there was an issue, I knew to pay attention.

Usually.

During this meeting, my mind kept wandering to Alicia and the prospect of being a father before I'd even gotten married. If I was the father to her baby, it would mean a life-time of responsibility and connection to her and the child that was not of my own choosing. Yes, I had slept with her several times, but I hadn't taken it beyond sex, and she didn't seem too concerned when we split. Had I been so wrong? Or was it just one of those flukes of fate where one false move, one tiny slip in concentration and boom. Your life goes in a totally different direction.

I just couldn't believe that the moment of contact Alicia and I had during sex was enough to get her pregnant. It had to be wishful thinking on her part.

I stared at the report in my hand and replayed the night I'd spent with Alicia over in my mind, focusing in on that moment when she was on top of me and I thought she would only kiss me and not try to actually ride me. When I felt her body press against the head of my dick, it felt incredible, but at the same time, alarm bells rang out in my head and I actually lifted her up and off of me, joking that she was getting carried away. I had grabbed a condom and slipped it on, and we continued where we left off. Could that tiny moment of contact have been enough? If my dick entered her body, it wasn't more than an inch. That would have to be the unluckiest inch ever to have entered a woman's body if so.

No. I was certain that I wasn't the father and that Alicia was just desperate to have someone -- anyone -- on the hook to help her. How much more desirable as a baby daddy was I compared to her other prospects? She worked in the financial industry in marketing -- some low-level job -- and so she wouldn't be able to provide a really good life for the child. Someone like me would be a boon for her because I would have to ensure the child had the very best of everything in keeping with my own level of income. That could only benefit Alicia.

I noticed the room was silent and glanced up from my document, the image of Alicia pushing a stroller dissipating when I saw that everyone was looking at me expectantly.

I hadn't even heard the question.

"Sorry," I said. "I was thinking of something else. What was the question?"

Keith cleared his throat and explained what he'd been talking about and repeated the question. I made sure to keep my focus for the rest of the meeting, pushing thoughts of Alicia and the baby out of my mind at least for the rest of the meeting.

When it was over, Keith came over to me as I was gathering up my materials.

"Hey, boss, do you want to get a drink and talk about whatever you were focused on in the meeting? We haven't been out for happy hour for weeks and weeks."

I exhaled and smiled at him. "You know, I'm glad you asked. I need a drink."

"Then I'm your man. I'll even buy the first round. Meet you downstairs? We should go to McNally's since it's so close."

"McNally's it is."

I went back to my office and after speaking with my assistant about the next day's work schedule, I grabbed my jacket and scarf, ready to go meet Keith for a drink. Before I left, I thumbed a message to Ella to let her know I'd be out for a drink with Keith.

JOSH: Hey, there, pretty lady. Just a text to let you know that I'm going to McNally's for a beer with Keith and some commiseration about things. See you in an hour or so.

ELLA: Hey, handsome gentleman. Back at you. Have a nice time. I'll be fixing dinner in that case. Would you prefer left-over Chinese or leftover Chinese?

JOSH: I think I'd prefer leftover Chinese, if you wouldn't mind. See you in an hour or so.

ELLA: See you. XOXO

JOSH: OXOX

I put my cell away and took the elevator to the lobby, the stress of the day already seeping out of me with each foot the elevator traveled. When the elevator doors opened and I saw the fading light of day, the streetlights already switching on, I couldn't wait to get outside and walk in the cold air. The bar was about a dozen blocks away. It would revive me after a day spent inside stuffy offices and meetings.

On the street, I saw Keith ahead of me and so I ran to catch up with him.

"Good timing," I said when I reached his side.

He reached out and patted me on the back. "What's got you so distracted? You look like a man in need of a serious drink or two. "

"I am," I said and smiled. "Lots of stuff on my plate and a few are pieces of shit."

"That's no good. We'll remedy that with beer. I found it doesn't make the pieces of shit go away, but it does make them more bearable for a couple of hours."

We entered McNally's and the noise of the patrons and the smell of beer and food put me in a good mood already.

Keith had his coat off already and hung it on a nearby coat rack, before grabbing a bar stool. I joined him, removing my coat and then sitting on his left. Behind us, the Knicks pre-game show played on a flatscreen, the talking heads showing highlights of previous games. The bartender came over right away and took our orders.

I watched while he grabbed the beers out of a cooler and removed the lids, placing them in front of us.

Keith and I both grabbed our beers and held them up in a toast to each other.

"To dealing with shit through alcohol," he said and gave me a grin.

"To alcohol," I replied. We each took a long draw at the beer and then I exhaled and closed my eyes, enjoying both the flavor of the imported beer and the cold feel of it rolling down my throat.

"Ahh," I said and took in a deep breath. "That's better. And this," I said and took another long pull. "This is even better."

"One of those nights, is it?" Keith asked. "Trouble with the little lady?"

I shook my head. "Ella? No. Not at all. She's fantastic. She's wonderful. It's another thing."

"What thing? You can tell me."

I chewed my lip, wondering if I could tell Keith. Then I figured -- what the hell. He's my only real friend outside of my brothers.

"This girl I fucked back before I met Ella? One after Christie and I split? She got a court ordered paternity test and named me as a potential father."

"What the fuck?" Keith said, his brow furrowed. "Who is she? Do I know her?"

"You and I were out at the WS Club and we both met these two really nice-looking women. Her name is Alicia Conroy, and you were with her friend, Marcy."

"Oh, I remember that night," Keith said, his voice trailing off. "Marcy was pretty hot. Brunette with big tits. We had a few dates, but nothing came of it. That's like the worst luck in the world."

"Yeah, my thoughts exactly."

"You had unprotected sex?"

I shook my head. "I always use a condom, but Alicia kinda got on top of me before I could get one on and for a brief, very brief, three or four seconds, she sat on me. I stopped her and rectified the situation, but I guess she figures it was long enough for me to be the father. Anyway, I'm going down to a lab to get tested on Tuesday. I should know one way or the other by Friday next week."

"I can see why you were distracted today during the meeting."

"Yeah, it's kind of hard to focus when you're wondering if you're going to be a daddy to some woman you barely know."

"Does Ella know?"

"Yes," I said and took another sip. "I told her right away."

"How did she take it?" Keith asked, making a face of sympathy.

"She was perfect about it. No problem on that front," I replied, feeling relieved at how she dealt with it. "But still. It's kind of sucking the joy out of our plans for our wedding on Easter Saturday."

"I guess," Keith replied and we turned around and sat staring at the flatscreen for a moment in thought. "Maybe it won't be positive, and you can just put all this behind you."

"I hope so," I said. "But it sucks the big one and not in a good way that we even have to worry about it. At least the wait will be short."

"There's that. Nothing to do but cross your fingers or pray, if you're into that kind of thing."

"I'm not really the praying type, but I'm reconsidering. If it would help, I'd be on my knees in a flash."

"Well, I'm the praying type, so I'll put in a good word for you."

I smiled. "I can use all the help I can get."

The first beer finished, we ordered a second. That one went down pretty easily and so we ordered another. I checked my cell and saw that it was already close to seven thirty.

"I have to get back," I said and took a deep pull on my beer. "My lady love is fixing up some mean leftover Chinese takeout for supper. Don't want to keep her waiting. Plus, the game starts soon."

"Say hello to her for me. I think I'll stay and finish this one, watch some of the game."

"Okay," I said and went to the coat tree to grab my coat and scarf. I put them on and went back to Keith, who had turned around on his bar stool and was watching the flatscreen behind us. "Thanks for being a sounding board for my troubles," I said and patted him on the back.

He extended his hand and we shook. "Don't mention it. I consult on all matters of the heart, big or small."

"See you tomorrow," I said.

I left the bar, walking down the street towards the building and the love of my life. I needed the crisp night air to ward off some of the alcohol and was glad to have a dozen blocks to walk to refresh myself after two and a half beers. I could hold my alcohol with the best of them, but they had been fast, and I knew my blood levels would be close to the line, so it was a good thing I didn't take my car.

I stared up at my building and saw the lights of the penthouse were on, the glow from inside a warm yellow.

Despite the impending chance of bad news, I felt incredibly happy to have Ella waiting for me.

I took out my cell and sent off a text to Ella, so she knew I was on my way home.

JOSH: Hello, my beautiful fiancée. I'm just walking towards the building after two and a half beers with Keith, crying into my beer about my hard luck with you know what. I'll be there momentarily, craving your affection and some reheated day-old take-out fried rice and beef with broccoli.

ELLA: I'll be waiting with bated breath for your presence...

I laughed, glad to be blessed with a beautiful woman, smart, accomplished and with a great sense of humor.

When I finally arrived at the building, I said hello to the night security guard and took the elevator up to the penthouse. I was unwinding my scarf and unbuttoning my jacket when the elevator doors finally opened. There, waiting for me, was my love, dressed in nothing but a tiny frilly apron around her waist, and a smile. I went right over to her and pulled her into my arms for a kiss, squeezing one buttock when I did, enjoying the creamy smoothness of it.

"What about reheated day-old Chinese take-out?" I asked, nuzzling her neck, one hand squeezing her breast.

"It can wait," was all she said, her voice throaty. She turned around and I followed her to the bedroom, my hands grabbing her naked buttocks.

15

ELLA

I STEWED THE REST OF THE WEEK, UNABLE TO GET Krista's words out of my mind. I decided to talk with Maryanne in HR and see if I could get a better idea of how people moved up in the company and what qualifications they usually had in order to be an editorial assistant. Maryanne was a middle-aged woman with perfectly styled blonde hair and rose-colored eye glass frames. Dressed smartly in a suit that seemed to be inspired by Dior, she was very professional looking.

"Hi, Maryanne," I said and sat down at the chair in front of her desk. "Thanks for agreeing to see me without an appointment. I wanted to ask a few questions about jobs at Dominion."

"Ask away? What are you interested in?"

"What does it take to get hired as an editorial assistant?"

She pursed her lips and considered. "Usually, some experience in the book publishing business and some familiarity with the editorial process, experience editing at some level."

"Do you usually look for an MA in English?"

"It's a bonus but not a requirement, if the other qualifications are exemplary." While she talked, she went over to a filing cabinet against the wall and searched through some files. She found one and pulled it out, bringing it back to the desk.

She opened it up and I saw that it was my HR file.

"For example, you have a degree in English from Dartmouth. That's impressive. It's an Ivy League college and so it carries a lot of weight. You were also the editor of the *Stonefence Review*, which is a notable student literary journal. You had a couple of short stories published as well. That's a great resume for someone hoping to go into book publishing."

"So, it's not unfair that I am going to be an editorial assistant in May?"

"No, of course not. Why would you think that?"

I shrugged, not wanting to mention Krista. "I didn't want to be seen as getting the job without being properly qualified."

"Did someone make you think that?" she asked, frowning, her hands folded on the desktop. "Tell me who and I'll speak with them."

"No, it's okay. I just didn't want people to resent me for getting the job after only four months."

"Did someone say something to you?"

I shrugged, not wanting to actually name Krista. "I heard a whisper, and that's all I'm going to say."

She leaned back in her chair. "Don't think you were hired because of Josh for a second. We were lucky to get you as an intern. That's why Sharon hired you on the spot when you asked if the job was still available."

"I thought it was because she had no one for two weeks and was desperate."

"That, too, but you shouldn't discount your credentials. Ivy League degrees and experience editing a literary magazine are not bad for a starting resume. You were a catch. Don't forget it. You and Josh marrying won't diminish that."

"Good," I said. "I just don't want the staff to resent me, and think that I got where I get because of my relationship to Josh."

"You didn't have that relationship when we hired you. As long as you don't screw up majorly, you should be fine. Don't let the naysayers get you down. In this life, they will always be there, trying to undermine your confidence. If you doubt yourself, they win." She closed the file on the desk and gave me a firm nod. "Don't let them win."

"I'll try not to," I said and exhaled, telling myself that her words were wise. Krista was just jealous. People were going to be jealous of me because I met and was marrying Josh, one of the richest eligible bachelors in Manhattan. I couldn't let them get in the way of my happiness.

I was determined not to let the haters win.

That weekend, a blizzard hit the whole eastern seaboard as the Polar Vortex swept down and engulfed the region in a blast of cold air. Josh and I stayed in the penthouse and watched sports and new movies on Apple TV. I had my period and was somewhat crampy, so I drank extra red wine, which seemed to lessen my cramps. It wasn't a very sexy weekend for us, but luckily, we got some loving in the previous week. Both of us had needed extra affection and sexual release, probably due to the stress of the coming paternity test. On Sunday night, we snuggled on the sofa and I finished my second glass of red wine.

"You getting drunk tonight, are you?" Josh asked as he poured me more.

"Drowning my cramps," I said and held up my glass in a toast. He held up his bottle of beer and we clinked together.

"I'll join you and drown my sorrows in beer."

"What sorrows could you possibly have, Mr. Macintyre?"

"Other than fears that I'm an accidental father, you mean?"

"You have me," I said, my brain feeling a bit fuzzy from two big glasses of wine. "You have a new penthouse apartment that will be renovated according to your preferences. You have a newspaper that you are re-creating from the ground up. You're set to get access to several million dollars as soon as we get married with which you can hire even more staff and make the *Chronicle* even better."

"You're right," Josh said and leaned back, his head against the back of the sofa, his eyes closed. He rubbed the bridge of his nose and then turned his head to look in my eyes. "I'm damn lucky and I know it. This glitch, even if it turns out bad, is just a small speck on an otherwise-wonderful life." He smiled and I couldn't help but smile back at his large blue eyes, which were warm. "I love you, Ella."

I leaned closer, my arm around on the back of the sofa. "I love you, Josh. Whatever happens this week, we're in this together."

"We are," he said, and we kissed. "That means the world to me. I want us to be totally honest with each other and open with everything -- every fear and doubt and worry."

"And every bit of happiness, too," I said, remembering Maryanne's words from the day I met with her.

"Yes, every bit of happiness. We have every right to be over the moon," he said and rubbed my cheek. "No matter what happens with the test, you're everything I could have ever dreamed of in a partner."

I smiled and kissed him again, my heart swelling with happiness.

Then, I remembered my discussions with Maryanne and decided it was time to tell Josh what happened. I didn't want to get Krista in trouble, but he did want me to be completely honest. It was something that had upset me so if I wanted to remain true to our pledge to each other, I had to come clean.

"There's something I've been meaning to talk with you about and now is as good a time as any," I said and played with the collar on his t-shirt.

"What's up?" he asked, his brow furrowing. "Something wrong at work?"

I shrugged, wanting to downplay it. "Nothing, really. Just something someone said to me after a meeting. This other employee suggested that I got the job as an editorial assistant because of my connection to you. It upset me so I went to see Maryanne in HR to talk about the usual qualifications for the position."

"And?" Josh said, his eyebrows raised. "I'm sure Maryanne set you straight."

"She did. She said that I was more than qualified as an editorial assistant, especially after working for Dominion for six months."

"Exactly," Josh said and pulled me closer. "We're lucky to have you. Don't ever doubt yourself. You went to Dartmouth. That's *choice*. You edited the literary journal. You're even published. When Sharon hired you, she told me she'd snagged a real gem. She was right."

He kissed me and I couldn't help but feel warmth well up inside of me at his words.

"In fact, she wasn't the only one to find a gem. I found one, too. It cost me scraped elbows and knees, but it was worth every moment of pain."

He smiled and held my gaze, and I teared up at the sentiment. "What would have happened if I didn't jaywalk that first day? I might never have met you in a way that would lead to us becoming instantly intimate."

"I know. Twists of fate are amazing. I'm glad we had ours or life would have been completely different. I would have been trying to find a partner using Marcella's service and being disappointed with every person I met. I would have been going to clubs and bars with Keith and company, trying to meet Ms. Right and failing because unless you were there, she wouldn't be Ms. Right."

"Do you really believe that?" I asked, feeling uncertain, although I was flattered. "Do you really believe you would still be single?"

"No one has compared to you," Josh said and pulled me into his arms, so that I lay across his lap, my arms around his neck. "No one could. You're everything I want. Everything I need. It's like you were made for me. Perfect fit."

I smiled and closed my eyes when he kissed my neck. "You're everything to me and everything I could dream of."

"Good," Josh said and held his hands on the sides of my face, his eyes burning into mine. "Don't ever doubt my feelings for you. If you need me to tell you, I will happily. Every day of my life for the rest of my life."

I felt emotions well up inside of me. "I'd love to hear it every day. If you want, I'll tell you happily every day of my life for the rest of my life."

"I think we have our wedding vows."

I smiled. "You think so? We'll have to see what the officiant says but I agree."

"Speaking of which, who should we get to officiate? I'm failed Catholic. What are you -- failed Presbyterian?"

"Yep."

"I guess we should go with Presbyterian, because I think the penalties for being a failed member are less onerous to overcome if you want to get married."

"I thought you'd want to be married in a cathedral in Manhattan," I said, surprised that he was so willing to forgo a Catholic ceremony.

He shrugged. "I did at one time, but I don't expect you to become a Catholic. I'm not a good Catholic. I like the cathedrals and the pomp and ceremony, but more for theatrical purposes than religious. If my parents were still alive, I probably would want to coerce you into becoming Catholic and marrying me at St. Patrick's. In fact, I believe Marcella was going to book it for me, on the off-chance I found a bride through her matchmaking service."

"Oh, that's right," I said, remembering the whole business when we first met. "You had it all figured out."

He shook his head. "Yeah, I thought it would be so much easier to find a wife using her." He kissed me warmly and we snuggled together, our foreheads pressed against each other's. I couldn't help but tear up, remembering those first days when I was so new to Manhattan. It was like a dream to me at that point.

"I looked at the prospect of falling in love and finding my soul mate like it was a business project," Josh said and looked in my eyes. "I thought I'd have to go through date after date, interviewing potential fiancées, matching likes and dislikes, hopes for the future, backgrounds. Little did I know all it took was a couple of scraped knees..."

I smiled and laid my head against his shoulder, glad I had jaywalked that morning. It turned out to be the best mistake I had ever made.

The next day, in the middle of the morning when my head was in the middle of a manuscript that I particularly liked, my cell dinged indicating an incoming text.

I checked and saw it was a text from Steph.

STEPH: *Hey kiddo, I'm going to be in Manhattan for the weekend on Thursday night. I thought we could get together and shop for dresses on Friday and I could finally meet this mystery man who stole you away from me. I'll be returning to Concord at five o'clock on Sunday, but we'll have all day Friday and Saturday to enjoy.*

I smiled to myself, excited that she'd soon be in town and we could spend time together. If the news about Josh and the baby was bad, I'd need Steph to help me get through it. I'd always have her ear and could call or text her if I needed to sound off but having her in town would be a bonus.

ELLA: *I can't wait to see you. Where will you stay? You could stay at the apartment. There's a spare bedroom.*

STEPH: *Naw, I'm staying at a cute little Airbnb I found. It's already paid for so I can't back out due to the short timeline. Besides, I don't want to get in the way of your time with Mr. B -- for billionaire.*

ELLA: *He's really not a billionaire, Steph. He's worth millions, but not billions -- yet. His father didn't believe in inherited wealth.*

STEPH: *That's rare. Usually, rich people can't wait to make their own kids rich.*

ELLA: *His dad was a self-made man and believed in his sons making their own way in life, with his help of course, but they had to work for it. I wish you were staying with us.*

ELLA: *No. It's good I got the Airbnb. This way, I can enjoy the New York experience and see my bestie at the same time. Win-win!*

ELLA: *Okay, if you insist. I can't wait to see you!*

STEPH: *You get the big news today, right?*

ELLA: *Yes, and either way, I'm going to need to party this weekend so it's great timing on your part.*

STEPH: *I'll be here for you, no matter what the result is. Count on it. Talk later. Let me know what happens.*

ELLA: *I will. OXOXO*

STEPH: *XOXOX*

I smiled and put my cell away, glad I had such a good best friend. Whatever happened in my life, I knew she had my back.

Of course, I called Sharon right away and asked if I could take Friday off since Steph was going to be in town.

"I promise I'll make it up to you," I said. "I'll come in and work on the weekend next week. Put in the time."

"That's okay," Sharon said. "Have fun."

I leaned back in my chair and smiled, imagining the fun we'd have looking for dresses. This time, unlike the last, I knew I'd be wearing it for real instead of taking it back like I did with the dress I bought for the wedding I had planned but never went through with.

Although Josh and I had only known each other for a short time, I felt like I really knew him, knew his heart, and that made all the difference.

16

JOSH

Tuesday couldn't come soon enough.

On Tuesday morning, I tried to sneak out of bed without waking Ella, but as usual, she was a very light sleeper and her eyes opened when she felt movement.

I kissed her as she lay snuggled under the covers.

"Good morning, sleepyhead," I said and smiled as I nuzzled her. "Don't get up. I'm going for a ride."

"You're going this morning for the test, right?" she asked and stretched her arms over her head.

"I am," I said and sat on the side of the bed. "You still have an hour before you have to get up. "Go back to sleep. The alarm's set."

"Okay. Ride carefully."

I tucked the blankets around her and kissed her once more. Then, I got up, determined to get in a ride around Central Park first thing to clear my mind. I'd lain awake for hours the previous night, thinking through everything, worrying about the test results and what it would mean for me, for Ella and for my child. I hated the thought that my son or daughter would be raised separately from me.

I brushed my teeth and then dressed in my riding suit. Then, I filled a water bottle and slipped on my shoes and helmet before hitting the elevator button, my bike in hand.

As I took the elevator down to the lobby, I thought about my own life. I had loved my father deeply growing up and had been so privileged to have him with me my entire childhood and most of my adulthood. The thought of my son or daughter living with me as only a part-time father who only saw me on every third weekend was depressing. When I had imagined falling in love and getting married, it always included having children and being a father to them -- an involved father just like mine had been. Big dinners around a formal dining table, picking them up after school and doing baseball practice on the weekends. Teaching them how to do things, like change a tire or how to ride a bike. All the things my father had done for me. While I knew a mother could do those things just as well as I could, it would be my son or daughter.

I wanted to be in their life, no matter what.

It made me sad to think of a child growing up and not living with their biological father. Seeing me on weekends and alternating holidays -- or whatever arrangements we eventually made -- wasn't good enough.

I was determined that even if I couldn't live with my child, son or daughter, I would be the best father I could be, given the circumstances. I would make our time together special. I would prioritize spending time with them. It wouldn't be optimal, but it would be the very best it could be.

Outside, the streets were busy with early-morning pedestrians and cars were already backed up due to traffic. I hopped on my bike and started my journey around the park, the cold air waking me up. Overhead, the sky was clear, and soon, I'd be able to see the light from the sunrise. I decided to ride along the Hudson instead of the park, wanting to see the water. It wasn't very busy, so I had the lanes mostly to myself. The ride was meditative, and soon, I'd worked up a good sweat.

When I arrived back at the apartment, I was soaked and went right into the bathroom after parking my bike and removing my shoes and helmet.

"I have fresh coffee waiting and there's some bagels and fruit," Ella called out from the kitchen. "I'm on my way to the office."

"I'll stop by later," I called from the bathroom. "Before I go to the lab."

"Okay."

I had a quick shower and then dressed in a grey suit and white shirt, a black tie finishing the outfit. I went to the kitchen and ate a bagel with cream cheese and some of the fruit Ella had cut -- bananas, orange slices and pineapple. I filled my coffee thermos and then went down to my office, saying hello to my staff on the way. I popped my head into Keith's office and asked if we were still on for the three o'clock meeting.

"You're the boss," he said and glanced up from his computer screen.

"Okay," I said and held up my cup of coffee. "I have a meeting downtown this morning, but I'll be back after lunch. If you need me for anything, I'm always on my cell."

"Sounds good," he said and gave me a smile. "Something to do with MBC?"

"Nope," I said, clearly indicating with my tone I didn't have any intention of telling him the reason.

"Nuff said," he replied and held up a hand. He knew enough not to push further for an answer.

I sat at my desk for an hour and went over my agenda for the day, reading whatever documents my assistant had placed on my desktop for signing. About fifteen minutes before I planned to leave for my appointment at the lab, I checked my cell and saw I had a message from the rehab facility in California.

That couldn't be good. I checked my calendar and saw that Penny wasn't due to be finished her time there for another week.

I called the facility and spoke with the intake worker on duty at the front desk.

"Hello, this is Joshua Macintyre. Someone called me from your facility, but I missed the call when I was in the washroom."

"Oh, thanks for calling. We wanted to let you know that Penny left the facility before she finished her full treatment program. She had a lapse, and was unwilling to recommit to staying clean, so we asked her to leave."

"Oh, that's too bad," I said, a sinking feeling in my gut at the prospect she was using again.

"Relapses are common, and sometimes it takes several stays in rehab before an addict gets clean for good," the worker said.

"Did she leave a phone number or forwarding address?"

"No, unfortunately. She left her family's home address."

"I have that," I said. "Thanks for your help."

I hung up, a knot in my gut that Penny hadn't been successful in rehab. It was just one more thing to worry about.

I checked my watch. I had about five minutes before I needed to leave to make my appointment at the lab for the paternity test, so I grabbed my jacket and scarf and went down a floor to Dominion and Ella's office.

I knocked on her door and popped my head inside. "Hey, I'm getting ready to leave, but I wanted a snog first."

"Snog away," she said and turned away from the computer when I came around her desk, the door closed behind me. I reached down and pulled her up into my arms for a kiss. She slipped her arms around my neck and we connected for a long moment, and the feel of her body pressed against mine never failed to send a delicious jolt of lust to my dick.

"Mmm," I said and kissed her neck. "Auntie M almost gone for the month?" I asked, using her term for her monthly period.

"Soon," she said with a coy smile. "I'll be ready and willing by Thursday."

"I'll be more than ready and willing." I kissed her once more and released her. I went back to the door. "I'll talk to you later. Do you need me to pick up some more wine tonight?"

"Sure," she said and sat back down behind her desk. "Never hurts, just in case."

"See you."

She blew me a kiss and I mimed catching it and then sent it back with a smile.

I took the car and drove to the lab, which was located closer to Columbia University. I went inside and spoke with the receptionist, who had me fill out a form and provide my credit card information for billing purposes. Then, I sat in the waiting room and waited for them to call me. I took out my cell and checked my messages, but there was nothing beyond some spam that I deleted. I had to call Penny's family and see how she was doing and made a calendar entry with an alert to call later in the afternoon when I got back to the office.

Finally, a woman in a white lab coat stepped into the waiting room, a file in her hand.

"Mr. Macintyre?"

I stood and put my cell back into my pocket. "That's me," I said and went to where she stood.

"Please come with me. This will only take a couple of minutes."

I followed her down the hallway and into a room, much like a doctor's office room, with an examining table, some instruments and a chair used to take blood samples.

"Have a seat," she said and so I did, watching while she checked out a couple of vials on the counter. She went over my information to make sure I was the right person, and then she removed a vial and took out a stick which resembled a long cotton swab at the end of a wooden stick. "I'm going to have you open your mouth wide and will swab the inside of your cheek. This will collect some cells from the skin on your mouth."

"Okay," I said and opened wide. She took two samples and each time, slipped the swab inside a vial and closed it off. She wrote something on them and then she smiled at me.

"That's it. You can go now. Results usually take two business days, so you should hear back by Thursday."

"Thanks," I said and got up to leave. I thanked the receptionist and then went out of the building and back to my car.

It was one of the easiest tests I'd ever taken.

I drove back to the building and went to my office, glad to have that over with. Now, all I had to do was get through the next forty-eight hours and get the results. Hopefully, someone else was the father, and I would be free to plan my family instead of having it happen out of my control.

Keith came in for our three o'clock meeting and laid out a series of sheets of paper in front of me. He was my CFO and was updating me on the hack that had been discovered weeks earlier and which the IT department finally understood. I knew it wasn't good news when I saw the expression on Keith's face.

"Give it to me straight," I said and leaned back in my chair. "What's the damage?"

"Extensive," Keith said with a sigh. "We've had to totally clean all our servers and get new passwords for everyone and new protocols in place to protect our privacy. Someone -- a new staff member -- made the mistake of clicking on a link in an email that appeared official and the hacker got access to all our email and our servers. It's a nightmare."

"Do they have information that is mission critical? I mean, is there anything that might put us in jeopardy?"

"Can't be sure," Keith said. "That's why I suggested new servers and starting over. There was no way to be sure whoever hacked our servers didn't put some back door in that we aren't aware of. Don't want to find out after the fact."

"Who would want to hack us? What could they gain?"

Keith shrugged. "Extortion? Blackmail? Who can say? MBC has made a lot of enemies over the years. People whose crimes have been exposed to the public. Political scandals. Sex scandals. The company has dealt with it before, and we have a great legal team who knows how to deal with anything that comes up, but this is the digital age and it has new dangers."

We spent the next hour talking about the hack and everything that had been done to fix it.

"Will this stop someone from hacking us? I'd like to prevent it from happening again."

"Can't make that promise," Keith said. "It'll happen again. The hackers are the smartest people in the business and they're also the most excited to push the boundaries and the least likely to care about the fallout."

"I need a drink after that," I said. "Feel like going to Riley's for happy hour?"

"Twist my rubber arm," Keith said. "I'll meet you downstairs in the lobby at," he said and checked his watch. "Five thirty? I have a call in ten, but I should be done before then."

"Sounds good."

After Keith left, I called Ella, to let her know I was meeting Keith for a drink.

"Come if you want," I said. "Keith won't mind."

"No," Ella replied. "I'll go home and make supper. You come home when you're ready, and we'l watch the game."

"Oh, yeah," I said, remembering the game started at seven thirty. "I'll be home before the game starts. We can eat and watch."

"See you then."

I ended the call and spent the next forty-five minutes finishing up some work before going to meet Keith for a drink.

I needed to relax after that day and a drink with Keith and dinner and a game with my love was just the right medicine.

17

ELLA

JOSH RETURNED AFTER HIS HAPPY HOUR VISIT WITH Keith and had dinner with me. I felt like something savory, comfort food, so I made a dish that my mother used to make for me when I was home sick with a cold or flu -- creamy chicken pasta with broccoli and mushrooms. I even bought a small carton of this really expensive chocolate ice cream. My cramps were still pretty bad, so I needed to pamper myself. Wine would help, too, and luckily, Josh brought a bottle with him.

We had dinner in front of the television and watched the Knicks game, and it was only when the game ended, that we really got the chance to talk.

I told him about Steph coming for a long weekend as we were standing side by side at the bathroom sinks, brushing our teeth before bed.

"What's the occasion or is it just an excuse to get together?"

"We plan to spend the weekend shopping for a wedding dress and stuff for the penthouse."

"That's good," Josh said, nodding. "I'll finally get to meet the famed Bestie. Do you think I'll pass muster?"

"You already have," I said. "She's the one who talked me into going to meet you for the meatballs, so I credit her with our romance."

"I already love her, then," Josh said with a laugh.

"So, what happened of interest today at work?" I asked.

"Oh," he said and hit his head, his eyes closed. "I forgot to tell you. I got a call from the rehab facility in California. I guess Penny left the program with only a week left. She relapsed with another patient and just decided to leave rather than commit to detoxing and starting over. I would have paid for another six weeks, if that's what it took, but maybe she needs to hit rock bottom before she'll really be ready."

"I thought she had hit rock bottom," I said, sad at the thought that she was back on drugs.

"No, not quite. She never had to sell herself for her drugs. That would be really hitting rock bottom. Luckily, she had family and friends and had a job until recently that she managed to keep even when using. I'm afraid she's really going to crash this time -- bad."

"Oh, Josh, I'm so sorry."

He put his arm around me when we were both finished brushing and pulled me against him. "No, I'm sorry. It's me who has the drama in my life. First, it's the potential of being a father to another woman's baby. Now, it's a former sex partner who needs rehab. Oh, and did I tell you some hackers broke into MBC and stole a bunch of emails and other documents? We're just waiting for them to try to blackmail us or extort money from us."

"That's terrible," I said and frowned. "How did they break in?"

"It's called phishing. They mimicked an email from one of the System Admins and asked people to click the link and sign in. One of the new hires in finance was dumb enough to click the link and sign in. The hacker used her password to get into the system. Unfortunately, it was an admin who had access to her boss's email and so the hacker got access to some really important financial information."

"What can you do about it?"

Josh exhaled. "It forced us to get new servers and email clients."

I shook my head, thinking about how easy it was for hackers to get into a business's system. "Why would anyone want to do that? Do they think they'll get access to what you know about a particular story MBC is working on? Are they trying to get dirt on the company to hurt it?"

Josh shrugged and slipped into bed, holding the blanket open for me.

"Your guess is as good as mine. If it was blackmail, I'd think they would have done something by now but so far, nothing. I haven't received any threatening emails or demands for millions of dollars in bitcoin to be deposited into some account."

I crawled in beside him and he covered us both with the heavy down-filled blankets. They'd just been cleaned and smelled of dryer sheets. I reached over and turned off the light on the night table and then snuggled down into his arms. The sheets felt cool against my skin, but Josh's body was so warm.

It was comforting.

"Do you have to tell the police?"

Josh shrugged. "It's not a crime, unfortunately, until they try to extort us. If they do, I'll be on the phone, but until then, I'll just assume it was a kid trying his or her hand at hacking a big company. That's done all the time."

We lay in the darkness for a moment, and I closed my eyes. Then I remembered the tests and decided to broach the subject.

"One day down and one day closer to getting the verdict," I said and leaned my face up for a kiss. Josh complied, kissing me tenderly.

"I'll be so damn glad when this is all over," he said, his voice sounding exhausted.

"Me, too," I said. "What are you going to do about Penny?"

Josh exhaled heavily, clearly upset at this turn of events. "Whatever it takes," he said finally. "I'll make some calls, see if her parents know where she is. I'll offer to pay for another six weeks, when she's ready."

"That's so generous of you," I said and stroked his bare chest. "She's lucky to have you in her life."

"Maybe if I hadn't been so insensitive to her needs and mental health when we were fucking, she'd be better now."

I frowned. "Josh, you can't blame yourself. You told her you weren't interested in anything more than fun now and then and so she went into it with her eyes wide open. You can't help it if she was lying to you and herself about what she wanted."

"I shouldn't have used her," he said softly.

"She used you, too. If she couldn't handle casual sex, she shouldn't become involved."

Josh exhaled. "She didn't realize at the time that she couldn't handle it."

I nodded and could see the expression in his eyes even in the darkness of the room from the moonlight that flowed in from the window. It illuminated his face, making his eyes seem unusually large and haunted.

"It's not your fault. She fell in love with you and wanted more than you could give. It happens all the time, Josh, to men and women."

"I know how it feels to be on the receiving end of that and it doesn't feel good. I guess it was Karma coming back to bite me in the ass."

I squeezed him. "I know," I said and laid my head on his chest. "Me, too. Karma's a bitch. I know all about it."

"What did you ever do to deserve Jerkface?" Josh asked, pulling me closer.

I sighed and thought about my past. "I was stupid, that's what. I was naive. I was so caught up in how perfect our lives seemed that I didn't realize that Derek didn't really care about me. He cared about being the husband of Governor Carlson's only child and only daughter. I cared about being a wife to a very powerful up-and-coming lawyer who had designs on public office one day."

"No, you're wrong. You weren't wrong to be trusting. You have to trust in this life, or you'll never get close to another person. You have to take the risk of loving someone and having your heart broken or you'll never feel love or be loved."

I turned and looked at Josh. "That's so..."

"So, what?" Josh said, a slight touch of humor in his voice. "So romantic?"

"I was going to say, honest and open." I kissed him. "You do have to be open to love and love requires trust. I guess a broken heart is the price we pay for love."

"That it is," Josh replied, exhaling. We lay in silence for a while, both of us probably thinking about our past mistakes and our current good fortune at meeting each other. At least, that's what I was thinking.

"Good night, Josh," I said and kissed him before snuggling down beside him with my back to him. "I love you."

He spooned against me and kissed my shoulder. "Good night, my love," he said softly. "I love you more than anything."

I squeezed his hand against my chest and sighed, my heart swelling with love for him and happiness for how good everything was between us.

. . .

Thursday came, and I'd woken up several times in the night, unable to get back to sleep for a long time, wondering what the test results would be and whether Josh would be a father a lot sooner than either of us hoped. Plus, I was excited for Steph arriving and hoped we would be celebrating instead of commiserating about the results.

Josh must have left early for his bike ride and was careful not to wake me up because he was already gone when I finally dragged myself out of bed and went to the bathroom. After I had a shower, I went to the kitchen for my breakfast and found a sticky note from Josh stuck to the coffee maker.

ELLA: Couldn't sleep.
I've gone for an early ride.
I'll bring fresh bagels.
See you soon.
Love, J.

I checked my watch -- it was still early, so I made a pot of coffee and had an orange while I waited for Josh to come back to the apartment. Before he left, Josh brought the paper up, and so I had my coffee and read the headlines, eager for Josh to arrive back and for us to indulge in fresh bagels and cream cheese.

The front door finally opened and in Josh came, his helmet off, his hair soaked from his ride. It fell into his eyes in a very sexy way that made me want to run my fingers through it and brush it out of the way of his big blue eyes.

He smiled when he saw me and after parking his bike, he came right over and gave me a warm kiss.

"Good morning, Ms. Carlson. I'd hug you, but I'm in need of a shower. I'll be back in five."

"I'll have the bagels ready," I said and grabbed the bag from his hand, eager to get breakfast going.

While he showered, I prepared the bagels, and poured him a cup of coffee just the way he liked it.

Then, we sat side by side at the kitchen island and ate our bagels and had our coffee, reading the paper together, like we did every morning since we moved in together. We really were like an old married couple in that way, except it all felt new to me.

I loved it.

Once we were both ready, we took the elevator down together and kissed each other when it was time for Josh to get off.

"I'll talk to you later," he said, and I smiled and waved as the elevator doors closed.

I rode the rest of the way down to my floor alone, smiling to myself. Then, I went to my office and sat behind my desk, ready for another day at Dominion. I realized, as I sat at my desk and glanced around my office, that I was truly exceptionally lucky. I'd recovered from a bad broken heart after Jerkface and I broke up, I'd graduated and moved to Manhattan with my dream opportunity as a slush reader in hand, and then I'd met Josh -- one of the most eligible bachelors in Manhattan -- all in the space of five months.

It was like a dream – one I hoped I kept dreaming.

18

JOSH

Thursday could not come fast enough.

Although I dreaded the news, I wanted to get it over with so I could deal with it and move on. Waiting was torture and as the hours ticked past, I sat at my desk and tried to focus on the reports from various departments at MBC to distract myself.

Finally, at around eleven thirty in the morning, after I'd gone for a long bike ride along the Hudson to clear my mind and kill time, I received an email from the lab. I sat and stared at the mail icon for a moment, trying to prepare myself for the news.

I kicked myself for being reluctant to open it. I'd seen combat in Afghanistan. I'd been through the deaths of both my parents and the breakup of an engagement.

By comparison, this was serious, but not the end of the world.

I opened the email and read the contents, my breath held.

. . .

Dear *Mr. Macintyre:*

Based on the results of our analysis of your DNA sample, we conclude that there is 0% likelihood that you are the father of the child. If you have any questions regarding this result, please feel free to call the office. One of our customer support team workers would be glad to answer them.

Sincerely,

Dr. James Fillmore

I leaned back in my chair and covered my face with my hands.

"Oh, thank *God,*" I said to the room.

As the stress drained out of me, I felt a small tinge of regret. Although I didn't want to be the father to this child, I had mentally prepared myself to be the best father I could be to him or her and had even imagined holding my child after she or he was born. But Ella and I would have our own children one day -- hopefully soon. My desire to have a family would be satisfied with her.

I felt bad for Alicia. She'd figure out who the father was, and it would hopefully be someone responsible enough to look after her and the baby.

The first thing I did was call Ella. She answered her cell right away, probably knowing this call meant I had the results.

"Hi, Sweetie," I said. "I'm not the father."

I heard her exhale on the other end of the line.

"Thank *God*, Josh. I mean, I feel bad for this Alicia person but glad for us."

"I know," I said, relief making me feel giddy. "I feel bad for her, too, but now we can put this behind us and focus on our future. We'll have our own children when the time is right."

"Yes," she said, and she sounded really happy. "We will."

"Well, that's all I had to tell you. Shall we go out for lunch and celebrate?"

"That sounds perfect. Pick me up when you're ready."

"See you at around twelve thirty," I said after checking my schedule. "We'll go get some deli food at Maxine's. I want a huge pastrami on rye and some of those great fries."

"I can't wait," Ella said. "I love you, Josh. I'm so relieved."

"Me, too," I replied. "I love you, Ella."

Then, we hung up and I sat back in my chair and let out a huge sigh of relief. It had been incredibly stressful, waiting for the news about the test. I had been prepared to be a father, but the truth was that I had a lot of living to do before I wanted children. I had a new penthouse renovation to finish, I had a wedding to arrange, and I had a honeymoon with my love to plan. Plus, I had a paper to run and an empire to manage. Having a child was not on my radar for at least a year or more, depending on what Ella wanted.

She had her own plans. She wanted to work as an editorial assistant and when she got enough experience, move up to a full editor. She wanted to write her own novel and get a publishing contract. She wanted us to live together and travel. She wanted children as well and hopefully, when the time came, she'd have that as well.

We had our whole lives ahead of us and now that this one potential speed bump had passed, there was nothing else in our way.

At twelve thirty, I grabbed my coat and scarf and took the elevator down to Ella's office to pick her up. She smiled when I entered her office and closed her laptop, grabbing her bag from the drawer in her desk.

"There you are," she said and came over to me. She slipped her arms around my neck. "Give me a kiss."

I was only too happy to oblige, grabbing her and picking her up off the floor. We kissed, deeply, and I felt an over-whelming love for her at that moment.

I was so lucky, and I knew it.

"Let's go get some pastrami," I said and helped her with her coat and scarf. "I'm so hungry I could eat half a cow."

"Me, too," she said, her eyes wide. "Although maybe only a quarter." She grinned at me and I put my arm around her shoulder, squeezing.

We walked out together, my arm still around her posses-sively, and I didn't care who saw us giving a PDA. She was going to be my wife and to hell with what anyone thought about it.

The deli was only eight blocks away from the office, so we elected to walk there, hand in hand.

"Aren't you glad we no longer have Reg and crew tailing us?" she asked.

"Yes, but I do miss someone else doing the driving," I said and smiled down at her. "I kinda like the whole limo thing."

"Do you really?" she asked, frowning.

"Yes," I replied. "I hate Manhattan traffic. I'm happy when someone else has to worry about it."

"So, use the limo service all the time," Ella offered. "You can afford it and it employs people."

"That's the ticket -- I can justify it by saying it boosts the economy," I said with a laugh. I glanced down at her smiling face. "I like the way you think."

We kissed and then arrived at the restaurant. It was busy and the lineup extended out the door.

"I guess we have to wait for a table," I said. "Everyone else seems to have the same idea as us."

"I can wait," Ella said and stood beside me. "Their pastrami on rye is the best."

While we waited, we discussed the renovation and where we were at.

"They're finishing the new drywall this week and the floors. Once the new fixtures are in, we can start picking furniture."

"Steph's coming today, right?" I asked, remembering Ella telling me that Steph was coming for a stay. "You two can go out and shop together."

"I want us to pick stuff out, too," Ella said, a touch of protest in her voice.

"Oh, sure, we will," I said. "All the big stuff. Sofa, television, sound system. But you two can pick out all the decorations and smaller stuff. I don't have to okay everything. I trust your taste."

"We're probably going to focus on the wedding dress and bridesmaid dress," Ella said. "Of course, I'll show you my choices, but she has to pick out her own dress. That was her one requirement."

I smiled. "I can't wait to finally meet her. The mythical Steph has loomed large in my life since I met you."

"She's tall and doesn't want anything to make her look taller and as she called it, giraffe-like."

"How tall is she?"

"She's probably almost six feet. She played basketball."

"That's tall for a woman," I said, picturing her in my mind based on photos Ella had shown me.

"She's been self-conscious about her height all her life," Ella said.

Just then, our table opened, and we went to it, glad to finally be inside. We removed our coats and sat at the table, taking the menus the waitress offered, even though we both knew what we wanted to eat.

We placed our order and then sat back, looking at each other, both of us smiling.

"I'm so happy," Ella said and reached out to take my hand. "I was trying to psych myself into being a step-mother, and I was ready to accept it if you were the father, but I'm so glad you're not."

"I feel incredible relief that a one-moment lapse didn't make me a father before I wanted to be."

"I hope everything works out for her," Ella said softly, and I loved her for her empathy.

"Me, too, but right now, I want to talk about us. Will we go to the penthouse with Steph and show her the place?"

"She'd love that," Ella said. "I'm so happy you'll finally meet her. We'll take her out for dinner and then drop by the penthouse. How does that sound?"

"Sounds good. Where should we go?"

"She wants meatballs," Ella said with a laugh. "She encouraged me to meet you for dinner that first time and now she wants to have them herself."

I laughed and kissed her knuckles. "It's quite the love story."

"It is. It has a happy ending, too."

"It does."

We had a nice lunch, chatting as we did about everything -- the penthouse, the wedding, Steph's visit.

When lunch was over, we walked back to the office and I kissed her goodbye, sending her off to her office while I went up to mine. For the rest of the afternoon, I kept busy with work and barely thought about anything but business. I was so relieved to have the paternity test out of the way that I could focus on the *Chronicle* in a way I hadn't been able to before I got the results.

One thing I did before the end of the day was to call the Ritz and reserve the same hotel room I did for Steph and Ella the last time Steph was in town. Steph could have stayed with us at the apartment, because we had an extra bedroom, but I knew it would be extra fun for them to stay at the Ritz. It was a treat for them both. It would give me a chance to work through the weekend, trying to get caught up with the issues arising from the data breach. I knew Ella would be happy, spending time with her best friend at the Ritz so it was money well spent.

S teph arrived just after six, and Ella met her in the lobby, too excited to wait for her to come up on her own. She brought her right up to the apartment where I was waiting. Ella was right -- Steph was tall, and pretty with long wavy blonde hair and hazel eyes. She was imposing but was quite attractive at the same time.

"Hello, Steph," I said and gave her a quick hug. "I'm so glad to finally meet you. Of course, Ella's talked about you pretty much from the first day we met. I've been so curious to finally meet you."

"Do I match her description? She tends to describe me as a gazelle, but I feel more like a giraffe."

"A thoroughbred is more what I was thinking, to be truthful," I said, for she did remind me of a racehorse, sleek, looking like they could run for hours.

"Ooh, I like that. A thoroughbred racehorse. That's miles better than a giraffe. Do you mind if I steal it?"

"Not at all. It's all yours," I said with a grin. "Ladies? I have a treat for you. Here," I said and handed Steph the room key to their hotel room at the Ritz. "This is for you both, so you'll really enjoy your stay."

Steph took the room key and stared at it, but then she stroked it in a comic way, her eyes mock-rolling back in her head.

"Oh, my God, Josh. You shouldn't have," Steph said. "But I'm glad you did. Did you know about this?" Steph asked and turned to Ella.

"No idea," Ella said and leaned up to kiss me. "Thank you."

I smiled. "My pleasure. This will give you two a chance to indulge yourselves and me to work all weekend."

"Not all weekend? Aren't we going out for dinner?"

"Absolutely, we're going out for some delicious meatballs. The best meatballs in all of Manhattan. Shall we?" I asked and held out both my arms, elbows crooked.

"Please," Steph said took my arm while Ella took the other. "I'm famished. The food on the road isn't the best by a long shot."

We left the building and made our way to the restaurant where I first took Ella and had a lovely meal, and I enjoyed listening to Steph and Ella reminisce about old times growing up together, living in a college dorm together. I knew that Ella and Steph would be busy all weekend, shopping for dresses for the wedding and furniture for the apartment. Which was good, because I had to deal with my own issues -- namely, the hack of MBC and the breach of our security.

I hoped things were back to normal now, and that our staff was being properly trained to recognize phishing attempts and not get trapped but with staff overturning frequently, that was a real challenge.

19

ELLA

I was really excited about my long weekend with Steph and knew the two of us would have a blast.

Josh was a prince for being generous enough to spring for another stay at the Ritz. We had a room identical to the last time we stayed, but down the hall so it was like old times. When we arrived, we found some beautiful flowers and chocolates waiting for us in the entry to the suite, as well as a chilled bottle of Moët et Chandon. The gifts were from Josh and so we opened the box of chocolates and picked out our favorites from the menu.

"This is so much fun," Steph said as she poured us some champagne and we ate chocolates. "I promised myself I'd be good all weekend and stick to my low-carb lifestyle but to hell with that. I'm not missing out on these chocolates."

We planned on spending the entire time pampering ourselves, shopping and eating all the room-service meals and restaurant meals we could.

"I'm going to have gained ten pounds by the time I go back on Sunday night," Steph said and rubbed her very flat belly.

"Yeah, right," I said, laughing.

On Friday, after sleeping in until ten o'clock, we had showers and then went down for brunch, gorging ourselves on the buffet of eggs, waffles, sausages, and every kind of brunch food you could imagine. After we sat and digested for a while over our coffees, we set off to stroll around Chelsea and check all the bridal salons. I tried on a dozen dresses, trying to get an idea of what kind of dress suited my figure and what suited my personality.

I modeled several choices for Steph, and she took pics on her cell so we could compare and discuss later with Josh at dinner. He would have a say, since he was paying for it. He insisted on paying for everything and I didn't argue, considering his wealth. My parents were well-off in an upper middle-class kind of way, but if we really were going to fly to California and have the ceremony at David's mansion in the Hollywood Hills, I figured Josh could foot the bill.

Still, I tried to keep it in the not-insane realm, and so we avoided some of the higher-end designer boutiques and shopped instead at what we both considered middle-of-the-road stores in terms of prices.

"White or ivory?" Steph asked, and held up the dress skirt of one dress against my face. "I think you're better with ivory than pure white. It goes better with your coloring."

"Ivory it is," I said, not being up on all the issues with coloring the way Steph was. I had light red hair, which some called auburn, and greenish hazel eyes and a healthy dose of freckles to go along with both. "Now, the question is, should I go modern or traditional?"

"You're getting married at David Macintyre's mansion so modern would be appropriate, if you like modern. But do what you want. If you want a more traditional gown, go for it."

I shrugged. I didn't know what I preferred. The only thing I knew was that I didn't suit something princess-like because of my height.

"I want something sleek, to make me look and feel taller. No puffy skirts or flouncy sleeves, as much as I love the princess look."

"Sleek and tall it is," Steph said and then, she acted as my consultant, selecting dresses for me to consider.

After four hours of going through dresses and through three different bridal shops, Steph found one that I immediately loved. It was vintage ivory lace embroidered on tulle, with a satin underdress. The bodice had a plunging V-neck, spaghetti straps, a form-fitting skirt, with a low v-back and tiny satin-covered buttons. The lace-tulle train extended about five feet.

It was a dream come true.

Steph snapped several pics of me in the dress standing on the platform and I had to admit I liked the way I looked in the dress.

"It's perfect," Steph said. "It's totally you, Ella."

"Am I too short for it?" I asked, biting my bottom lip.

"Not at all," Steph replied. "It elongates you because it's form fitting. You look stunning."

She actually had tears in her eyes as she stood there, taking pics and so I knew she really loved it.

There were several in stock, so I decided to show the pics we'd taken to Josh for his approval before I committed to it.

"Do you think Josh will like it?" I asked, although I knew he'd love anything that I did.

"He'll love it. You look like a model in it. Seriously. If you could grow a foot, you'd be perfect to model that dress."

I hugged her and we left, going to one more store before we were both exhausted. I found another dress that was about third best, in a similar silhouette but not quite as delicately embroidered as the one that I really loved. When we were finished, we went to a coffee shop and pored over the photos on Steph's cell and ate a donut while we considered.

"I really think this is the one," Steph said. "It's the best on you, and it's also the highest quality. The lace is beautiful and the buttons down the back? So nice."

"I'll show it to my mom and to Josh and see what they say. We still have time and could go out again. The seamstress said it would take six weeks to get the alternations done so we have time to decide and even go shopping for more choices if needed."

"Don't put it off too long. It's already late January. That leaves less than eleven weeks until your wedding, right?"

"That's lots of time. It's a low-key wedding, Steph. Just a ceremony at David's mansion, and then a honeymoon somewhere warm. Nothing big. Just family and closest friends. After the huge to-do about both Josh and my previous engagements, neither of us want to make this into anything ridiculous."

"I get that, but this is hopefully your one and only wedding. Try to make it exactly the way you want it to be. You both deserve it."

"We do," I said and took a long sip of my coffee. "Both of us were burned. We were both down on marriage and look what happened?"

"You found each other," Steph said. "And luckily, I encouraged you to go out for meatballs, or none of this would be happening."

I smiled and gave her a hug. "You're absolutely right. And if I had taken your advice and come home on the bus that day when I lost my briefcase?"

She nodded and shoved me playfully. "None of this would have happened. Okay, okay. You got me. I'm glad you stayed, and I'm glad I encouraged you to eat meatballs. In fact, that should be your motto -- the meatballs did it."

We laughed together and then decided to go back to the hotel and rest up before we met Josh for dinner.

Once we arrived back at the hotel, we both flopped down on the beds and watched some television for a while to decompress. I lay on the bed and scrolled through the images of me in various dresses, always returning to the one dress -- the vintage lace with the spaghetti straps and lace-embossed tulle overdress. It seemed appropriate for a small wedding and since the weather would be warm in

April in LA, it would be possible to wear it without freezing.

"Which dress, Steph? Was there one you liked so much, it would be worth not going out another day in search of just the right dress?"

"The last one," she said. "With the lace. I really liked it."

I remembered my last plan to get married with Jerkface and felt a little sick. We'd gotten far enough to have picked a venue, and even looked at wedding invitations. We were going to do the whole shebang -- big wedding with three hundred guests, married in a church, reception at a hotel in Concord, dance with live band. I'd spent weeks looking at dresses and trying to decide where to go for our honeymoon.

Then I saw Jerkface boinking Bunni on the desk and that was that.

"Am I making a mistake, agreeing to marry Josh so quickly?" I asked in a small voice.

"Yes," Steph said and I rolled over onto my stomach, my mouth open in shock.

"You really think so?" I said, my throat choking with emotion. "But I love him!"

"Yes, I think you should break up with him."

Then she rolled over on her own bed and glanced at me, a smirk on her face.

"Steph!" I said and threw a pillow over at her. "Don't even joke about it."

"Sweetheart, if I could talk you out of it, you would be making a mistake. You know in your heart that it's not a mistake. You're just thinking about Jerkface and the wedding that never was. Don't. That was then. This is now."

I exhaled and lay on my back, staring at the wedding dress. "You're right. I just wanted you to reassure me. I love Josh. He's such a good man. We have so much fun together. We don't want to be apart. *Ever.*"

"You're apart this weekend," Steph said.

"We mean, separated for any serious length of time. We want to live together and make our lives together and one day have a family."

"There," Steph said. "You've said it yourself. You love each other. You want to make your lives together and have a family. That's why you get married."

"It is," I said and put my cell down. "We both know what we want out of life. We just want to go for it together."

I rolled onto my stomach and watched Steph, who was filing her nails while lying on her back.

"Perfect," she said and sat up, dangling her legs over the side of the bed. "It's time to go meet Mr. Glutes and future Mr. Macintyre-Carlson for some food."

"Let's get ready."

The two of us got dressed and finished our makeup, and finally, I texted Josh to see if he was ready.

ELLA: We're hungry. Meet you downstairs like we planned?

There was a pause and I was curious why he didn't get right back to me. Finally, about five minutes later as Steph and I were sitting on the bed, watching local news, I got a text that made me frown.

JOSH: You two better go without me. Something came up that I have to deal with. Don't know how long I'll be, so go ahead and eat without me. I'm sorry about this but I have to deal with it. We'll have dinner tomorrow night okay? I'll text you later.

"Huh, that's weird," I said and texted him back. "Josh can't come right now. He says to go without him."

"Oh, that's too bad."

ELLA: No problem. See you tomorrow. Text me later so we can catch up.

I sent the text and shrugged.

I got off the bed and grabbed my bag then went to the door.

Steph came to my side and slipped her arm around my shoulders. "Well. Looks like it's just you and me, kid."

"That it does," I said and together, we went downstairs to the restaurant. "I hope everything's okay with Josh. He was kind of cryptic."

"That's text for you. Don't worry. I'm sure if it was really serious, he'd tell you. It's probably just something that came up at work he had to deal with at the last minute. These billionaires, you know. Always working."

"He's not a billionaire," I said, although I knew he would be one day unless things really fell apart.

"Okay, multi-millionaire," Steph said with a laugh, squeezing my shoulder. "If that makes you feel better."

"Just trying to be real," I said and pushed the elevator button. We rode down to the lobby and went to the restaurant, which wasn't a real restaurant, but was a bar that served appetizers that were so big and delicious, they could pass for full meals.

I wished Josh could be there with us, but it was fun being with Steph.

Luckily, we were able to get a nice table and were pampered by our waiter, who seemed really pleased to have a couple of young women to serve. Steph and I amused ourselves by examining all the guests and commenting on them all, trying to guess their occupations and life stories.

While I was happy to be there with Steph, I was so looking forward to being there with Josh, too, so they could get to know each other better.

That could wait. We had our whole lifetimes together.

20

JOSH

It was about quarter to six when everything went to shit.

I was sitting in my office, my head in a spreadsheet, trying to get a grip on financial projections for the paper, when Keith called. I figured he was just calling to say goodbye, because he was planning on leaving early and had already passed the request for time off by me.

"What's up? You getting ready to leave?"

"Head's up. Two FBI Special Agents just visited my office with a warrant. They've taken my computer and phone."

"What?"

"They had a warrant to search my office and take my computer and cell phone. I think they're with the Financial Crimes Division."

"Did they say what they were looking for?"

Keith exhaled heavily on the other line. "Evidence of MBC using offshore accounts to evade taxes and money laundering."

I rubbed my forehead, a sense of dread filling me. "Tax evasion? Money laundering? What's going on, Keith? You're CFO. What could they mean?"

"It means they think we're criminals."

"We've been audited for the past five years by the IRS. How could we be evading taxes? How did that supposedly take place? What offshore accounts? Whose money?"

"They claim we've been taking money from criminal enterprises, inflating the cost of purchases and making it look like the money was spent on renovations and purchasing equipment. Inflating the cost of services and using that to both launder money and avoid taxes."

"What criminal enterprises? What could we possibly be laundering money for? We're a news organization."

"They claim that someone in the organization is involved in a criminal enterprise and has been laundering money through the corporation."

"Who?'

"They say it's me or one of my staff," Keith said.

"For fuck's sake," I said and opened my door to see two men dressed in what was clearly FBI identified jackets walking rapidly down the hall towards my office. "I see them. They're coming down the hallway."

"Just cooperate. I've done nothing wrong, Josh. This will all be cleared up."

"Okay. Call my lawyer."

"Already did. Sullivan is on his way."

I ended the call and waited for the two FBI Special Agents to arrive, a very upset Jenna trailing behind them.

She tried to push by them. "Mr. Macintyre, I wanted to call you but they--"

"It's okay, Jenna. I'll take care of this. Go back to your desk."

Jenna nodded and dropped back, allowing the two Special Agents to come through.

"Mr. Joshua Macintyre?" one of the two men said. Older with thinning blond hair and piercing blue eyes, he was tall and lean, reminding me of an old cowpoke if you put him in a horseman's duster and cowboy hat instead of the FBI jacket. Beside him stood a trim younger man with dark hair and eyes.

"That's right. And you are?"

"Special Agent Stuart Thomas and this is my partner, Special Agent Glenn Woods. We're with the Financial Fraud Enforcement Task Force."

We shook hands and I led them into my office and offered them both a chair.

"I just spoke to my Chief Financial Officer, Keith Shepherd. He says you had a warrant to search his office and to seize his computer and business cell phone. Can you please tell me what this is about?"

The two men sat in the respective chairs and Special Agent Thomas cleared his throat. After adjusting his jacket, he glanced at me, his expression intense.

"We've received information that led to a Federal Judge issuing a search warrant for Mr. Shepherd's computer and cell. According to this information, MBC has been manipulating its accounts to avoid taxes for the past five years and hiding the money in illegal offshore accounts."

"That's impossible. We have been audited for the past five years by the IRS and each year, have been given a clean bill of health."

"Apparently, there was coordination with an officer in the IRS office in Manhattan. Here's the warrant."

Thomas placed a document on the desk in front of me. I glanced at it, noting that the warrant mentioned Keith by name and position and also mentioned several other people, whose names were redacted. It detailed actions Keith had taken to direct those working for him to falsify accounts.

"We wanted to ask you a few questions about Mr. Shepherd and his work for MBC," Thomas said.

"I'm afraid I'm going to have to speak to my lawyer before I can answer any questions."

"Fine," Thomas said. "You could come down to the Field Office on Monday and meet with us, with your lawyer present."

The two men stood, and Thomas handed me his business card.

"Call my office to arrange a time to come in."

"I'll do that."

They left and I sat down behind my desk, my gut in a knot. Jenna came running in after they'd left.

"I'm so sorry, Mr. Macintyre. I had no idea they were even in the building. They came in while I was in the washroom and--"

"Don't worry, Jenna," I said and waved my hand. "It's not your fault. They had a warrant to search Keith's office. There was nothing we could do. Go back to your desk. I'll take care of this. Send Mr. Sullivan down to my office when he arrives."

"I will," she said and left my office, closing the door behind her.

Just then, my cell chimed, and I checked it, remembering that I had promised to meet her and Steph for dinner and drinks at the Ritz. I begged off and told her something came up. She didn't need to worry about any of this until I knew more myself.

I sat for a moment with my head in my hands but glanced up when there came a knock at my door. Keith came in, shaking his head when his eyes met mine.

"I swear, Josh, I had no idea about any of this," he said and sat on the chair across from me, his face pale. "This is complete and utter bullshit. We haven't been evading taxes or laundering money. It's crazy. It's like we've been set up or something."

"I know," I said. "I'm thinking the same thing. Someone set us up and I think the hack has something to do with it. They hacked our servers and then probably used the hack to try to implicate us. We need access to those servers and all our data on the cloud. That should prove that we were above-board with all our financial deeds."

"Our hack was part of a larger attempt," Keith said. "I spoke with my guys in IT. Several other big news companies were also targeted, although not all of them were successfully breached. Whoever did this used pretty basic techniques to gain access to our email system, but then they were pretty damn expert in what they did after that. Our data was all corrupted. It had to be someone inside who could access our cloud data and then upload corrupted data. That's what the Feds got hold of. It's manufactured, Josh, to make us look like we were evading taxes and laundering money. But it should clear up fast, too, as long as we can prove that our system was hacked as part of a larger attempt to wipe out financial data and upload false data."

"Damn," I said. "What's with these hackers? So, we weren't the main target? It wasn't personal?"

"Who can say? Until we know who the hackers were, or who they were working for, it's impossible to tell. Trying to hack other news organizations might be cover to hit us without it being seen to be personal."

"In the meantime?" I asked, closing the file in front of me. "What do we do?"

"Cooperate with the Feds. We have no other choice, but we've done nothing wrong, Josh. I've done nothing wrong. You know you can trust me. We've been friends since college."

"I know I can trust you," I said, and I meant it. Keith was not only my CFO, he was a friend. "Let's just wait to see what our lawyers say about how to handle this. We'll do what they say. That's why we pay them the big bucks."

"Exactly," Keith said and exhaled, sounding relieved that I was being reasonable. Of course, there was no reason not to suspect he or someone in his department was cheating, but he was a friend and I trusted my instincts.

I hoped I wasn't wrong to do so.

Twenty minutes later, one of MBC's corporate lawyers, Trent Sullivan, arrived and came right into my office. His expression was grim, and I knew he was shocked at this turn of events. An older man with wispy grey hair, a silver goatee and thin metal glasses, he wore an impeccable three-piece suit. He'd been a corporate lawyer for years and he had worked for my father for most of the last decade. He knew the ins and outs of corporate law.

I went over to him and we shook hands.

"Thank God you're here," I said and ushered him to his chair. He took a seat and I went back around my desk and sat behind it.

"I heard about the hack through the grapevine but this visit by the FBI is a real shock," he said and removed his glasses, cleaning them with a kerchief retrieved from a pocket in his suit jacket.

"Tell me about it," I said and handed him the copy of the warrant the police and Feds had to search Keith's office and take evidence.

He finished cleaning his glasses and then read it over for a few moments, stroking his goatee while he did. "Yep. This is legit. I hope to hell Keith is telling the truth and he hasn't been screwing the company over all this time."

"I trust him," I said. "He's one of my oldest friends. I don't think he'd do this. He has a great income, stock options, great future ahead of him. Why would he jeopardize it by cooking the books?"

"Greed?" Trent leaned back in his chair and shook his head. "Unfortunately, I've seen it all before. People who think they're smarter than the Feds and the IRS. People whose desire for more -- money, sex, fame -- will do anything to increase their own bottom line. Sometimes, they have an addiction and get in over their heads and end up stealing from the corporation to cover debts."

"I never took Keith as someone who was reckless or deceitful. He's ambitious but he seems like he understands and respects the law."

"Let's hope so, for MBC's sake."

We discussed the possible outcomes for a while and finally, Keith showed up, knocking at the door.

"Come in," I called out when he popped his head inside. "Have a seat. Trent and I were just going over the warrant and what happens next."

"Good," Keith said and came over to shake Trent's hand. "Sorry you had to be called in on this."

"That's what you pay me to do," Trent said while Keith took a seat across from me.

Keith spent the next fifteen minutes going over the hack and what the IT and security people found, and then the arrival of the FinCEN people and FBI with their warrant.

"I'm going down on Monday to meet with the FBI to discuss the case," Keith said.

"Me as well."

"I'll come with you," Trent replied. "The three of us will meet before and go together. We can take the car to the FBI's field office for the interview."

"Sounds good." Keith stood up. "Is there anything else?"

"No, you're free to go forth and prepare. Try to get some rest this weekend so you're in top shape mentally on Monday."

"I'm really sorry about all this," Keith said. "But don't worry. There's nothing to find. If they get access to our original server, they can see how it was hacked and it must have been altered. There's no way there's any tax evasion or money laundering going on in my shop. None. If anything unlawful happened, I wasn't aware of it."

"I hope you're right," I said. "We just have to get through the next few weeks while they do the audit and hopefully, everything will clear up."

Keith said goodbye to Trent and on his part, Trent remained behind.

"Can you think of anyone who would try to hurt you by hacking MBC and planting false data?"

I shrugged. "I'm not an expert in this area of corporate espionage. I have no idea."

Trent nodded. "I'll talk to someone I know. Get him on the case. Maybe he can do some sleuthing and find out who might have a grudge."

"Thanks, Trent. I appreciate it. I know my father would be pleased to have you taking care of this, if he were still alive."

"I miss him," Trent said and shook my hand before slipping on his jacket. "He was such a force of nature."

"That he was," I said and thought about my father, who owned every room he walked into. He had very big shoes and I knew I'd never really fill them.

"I'll come by Monday morning. Until then, try not to worry too much."

"I'll try."

He left and I sat alone in my office for a few moments, trying to figure out what the hell was going on and who had it in for me and MBC...

21
***
ELLA

Friday night, after Steph and I went back to the hotel and lazed around, watching a movie on the movie channel and generally indulging ourselves in popcorn and candy, we went to bed with plans to shop until we dropped the next day.

Josh texted me late that night and it wasn't good news.

JOSH: Hey, how are you? Tired out after a day of shopping? Did you find anything you liked?

I smiled and texted back the photo of me in the dress I really liked.

JOSH: Oh, God, you look beautiful. Is that the dress?

ELLA: Maybe. We still have tomorrow to check out other stores, but it's one I liked the best.

JOSH: Well, it's beautiful. You look fantastic in it.

ELLA: How was your day? I missed snuggling with you and kissing you goodnight.

JOSH: *Not so good. Remember I told you about the hack? The FBI Financial Crimes Unit sent someone over with a warrant to search Keith's office and take his computer and cell.*

ELLA: *Oh, my God, Josh! What???*

JOSH: *Suspicion of tax evasion and money laundering. He has to go down to the office next week and answer questions.*

ELLA: *What are you going to do? He's your CFO for Dominion, right? Has he been cooking the books?*

JOSH: *He says it could be linked to the hack that took place a few weeks ago. Maybe someone planted incriminating evidence or something. We'll find out this week when both of us meet with the FBI's investigators.*

ELLA: *I'm so sorry... Why didn't you call me and tell me?*

JOSH: *I didn't want to ruin your weekend with Steph. I trust Keith, and don't believe he was cheating Dominion, but until we get to the bottom of this, things are going to be tense.*

ELLA: *I wish I was there with you right now.*

JOSH: *I'm fine. You go to sleep and have a good day with Steph. I shouldn't have even told you about this, but we made a pact to always tell each other everything that's going on. I didn't want to break that deal so soon after we made it.*

ELLA: *No, Josh, it's good you told me. I want to know when something happens with you. No matter what it is. Always tell me, even if it might upset me. We're partners.*

JOSH: *We are. That's why I told you, even though I wish you didn't have to know. Try not to let it bother you too much. I* don't want your weekend of fun and shopping with your bestie ruined.

ELLA: Don't worry. She and I have been through bad times and we've survived.

JOSH: Good. You better go to sleep now. Maybe we can meet for supper tomorrow.

ELLA: Sounds perfect. I love you. XOXOX

JOSH: I love you back. OXOXO

Then, I lay in bed and my mind went over everything -- the hack, the FBI visiting and taking Keith's computer and cell and files, the allegations of evading taxes and money laundering. It didn't seem right that Keith was cheating Josh out of money. They were friends in addition to being partners in the business. Keith was an executive for the publishing arm of MBC. It would be like me imagining that Steph was defrauding me.

On Saturday, Steph and I indulged ourselves in the luxury that was our suite at the Ritz-Carlton. Like the last time we stayed, we had a massage and facial at the spa and then spent the afternoon shopping for dresses but didn't find anything that I liked more than the dress from Friday. We also visited a couple of local furniture boutiques, picking out lamps and rugs and other things we'd need for the penthouse and taking photos of them so I could get Josh to approve. I could have bought them using the credit card Josh provided me in my name, but I didn't want to without him approving. When Josh and I had some time, we could go and check out the stores together and buy things for the penthouse. I couldn't wait for the builders to be finished with the interior renovations so Josh and I could get in and start decorating.

Saturday night, Steph and I met Josh for dinner at a local steakhouse, but the mood was subdued because of Josh's worry about the investigation. My own enjoyment of the weekend was as well and even Steph noticed it. On Sunday, we did the whole horse and buggy ride around Central Park and tried to enjoy the last few hours before Steph left to go back to Concord, but the anxiety I felt over the allegations put a damper on my fun.

I went with Steph to Penn Station where she was catching a train back to Concord and said a sad goodbye.

"The next time I see you, it'll be for the wedding," I said. "Get a dress for the wedding that you like and that you think suits you and send me the bill."

She gave me a big hug. "I had fun anyway. I know you were worried about Josh, but just getting away from home for the weekend was a great little holiday for me."

"Good," I said, and we hugged again. "I enjoyed it as much as I could, considering. Hopefully, this will all be cleared up soon and we can get back to normal."

She left me and went down the stairs to the platform and back to Concord.

I went back to the apartment and Josh.

M onday, Josh went to meet with the FBI and Justice Department prosecutors to discuss the case. I was on pins and needles all day, wondering what would happen.

I just couldn't believe that Keith was guilty of money laundering or MBC of illegally evading taxes. I was sure they would use every legitimate means to reduce their tax burden, as all corporations did, but to do it illegally didn't sound like the MBC I had learned of, especially not with Josh Sr at the helm. It had to be a mistake or industrial espionage -- someone trying to hurt MBC because of competition or out of a desire for revenge after MBC did a particularly hard-hitting story on them.

Of course, I thought about my father's partner and so I called my father up, hoping to speak with him.

When I told him about the case, he sounded concerned.

"I've always been resentful of MBC's coverage of the case," my father said, "but I would never do anything about it. There are probably dozens of people who have been targets of MBC's investigative reports on crime and white-collar corruption. Probably a few organized crime types as well. I guess the investigation should turn it up, if the evidence is there."

"I hope so," I said and sighed. "It's just another thing that's put a damper on our wedding plans. I hoped we could enjoy the next couple of months without anything hanging over our heads, but until this case is settled one way or the other, it's going to be a really stressful time for Josh."

"I'll do some calling, see what I can find out through my contacts, but if I were you, I'd just hunker down and keep busy, keep making your plans, and try to forget about it as much as possible. I've done some reading about Josh, and he's a solid, good man."

"He is, Daddy," I said, feeling relief that my father had finally seemed to come around to respecting Josh, even if he didn't really like the idea I was marrying into Josh's family because of his history. "He's a really good man and I love him. He loves me. I hate to see him so stressed like this, especially since he just started as CEO of MBC and none of its skeletons are about him or anything he's done."

"I get that. Unfortunately, he's inherited the corporation with all its warts. He has to deal with it now. Just try to be stoical about it until you get more information."

"Daddy, you're a natural stoic but the rest of us aren't. It's hard to be stoical when the chaos is all about you and yours."

"It's hard, but it's the best course of action. Try to focus on what's important -- each other. Let the FBI and DOJ do their work. If Josh is innocent, I'm sure it will come out."

"Okay," I said and exhaled. "I hope you're right."

"I'll call and let you know what I find out."

"Thanks," I said, and we said goodbye.

I got a call from Josh after lunch and he seemed in somewhat of a better mood than earlier in the morning.

"Hey, sweetie, how are you?"

"Forget about me," I said, anxious to hear what happened with the meeting. "How did the meeting go?"

"We had a very good meeting with DOJ and FBI about the case. They were very interested in the hack and thought it was suspicious. Luckily, we reported the hack to the appropriate officials and so they were able to check with our story and confirm the details. Looks like it was maybe -- maybe -- someone trying to set us up. They're looking at their source more closely now, so things are looking up."

"Oh, Josh, I'm so glad to hear that," I said, and a sense of relief flooded through me. "How come they didn't already know about the hack?

"Government's huge and one part doesn't always talk to the other parts," he replied. "They know now, so hopefully, this will be cleared up soon. I'm just glad they followed up on what we told them on Friday. Things are looking up with the case so I'm happy."

"Phew! I'm happy, too, in that case. I spoke with my dad this morning and he said he'd do some checking around, see what he could find out through his contacts. Josh, he said he thought you were a good solid man and that you wouldn't be involved in anything illegal."

"He did?" Josh replied, sounding pleasantly surprised. "Score! I figured this would sour your father on me, if he found out."

"No, he really seemed to be certain you weren't involved in anything criminal."

"That's a definite bonus, considering he's going to be my only father now."

"I know," I said. "The only question is who would be trying to get revenge on you and for what? I hope they find out soon, so we can move on with our lives."

"Me, too. Let's go out and celebrate tonight. What do you say?"

"There's a Knicks game today..."

"Oh, yeah. How about we stay in and celebrate tonight," he said with a laugh. "I'll pick up some Korean."

"Perfect."

We ended the call and I sat back in my chair, happy that the whole FBI DOJ business seemed like it might all be a tempest in a teapot.

J osh arrived at the apartment at around seven, bags of Korean takeout in hand. I went to him at the door and took the bags from his hands, while he removed his coat and boots. I had the coffee table set with plates and cutlery and napkins, so we could sit down and watch the game, which was recorded from earlier in the day.

I went to the refrigerator and took out a couple of Korean beers and opened them for us. Josh came over and took one from me and we kissed.

"Thank you," he said. "For everything."

"Thank *you*," I replied. We clinked the necks together and then took a sip before sitting down and dishing out the food.

"You don't mind that we're staying in?" Josh asked, while he scooped out some rice onto his plate.

"I don't mind at all," I said. "All that matters is that we're together."

"That's true," he said and leaned over to kiss me once more."

It was true. I was so glad my father seemed to have come around towards Josh. He really was a good man and once more, I was thankful for how my life had changed for the better when I moved to Manhattan. But I was also aware of how fragile it all was and how much luck played into my life.

If I hadn't crossed the street that morning, I would never have run into Josh and met the love of my life.

I watched him dishing out the Korean Spicy Beef Barbecue and tried to do just what my father advised.

Focus on each other. In the end, that was all that really mattered.

22

JOSH

THE NEXT WEEKS WHILE WE WAITED FOR THE RESULTS of the FBI investigation into the hack were tense, but I felt better and better as each day went by and the news from the FBI was good. I felt less and less stressed that Keith or one of his staff had been cooking the books without his knowledge.

While Ella and I waited for the final verdict, we tried to focus on the upcoming wedding in California and the renovation to the penthouse we bought. But it wasn't easy -- the length of time it took the FBI and DOJ to look into the hack and determine whether we were set up was excruciating. I wanted to put it in the past as soon as possible.

While we waited, we spent our time when we weren't working getting the wedding arranged with David in Los Angeles. He was excited to be hosting the wedding and spent a great deal of time on the phone with us, on Skype, showing us where we might hold the ceremony on his property overlooking the valley.

"Here," he said and held up his cell, showing us a panorama of the LA scenery spread out below his property, which was on the top of a hill. "You can see the entire city from up here. It's fantastic. We could put the table here and hold the ceremony over here."

He went to a spot below a large tree and I had to agree that it looked like it would be the perfect location for us to say our vows.

"I like it," Ella said and squeezed my hand. "I can see it in my mind's eye. It will be perfect. Thanks David."

"My pleasure," he said, and I could tell David was truly pleased to be hosting the wedding. He was as excited as a kid at the Disney Store for the first time.

"The weather will be beautiful and so we can plan to hold an afternoon ceremony followed by a dinner on the patio. I'll volunteer to grill some seafood and steaks for us if you like."

"No, no, David," I said and shook my head. "We can cater the food so we can all just sit back and enjoy the night."

"If you want, but seriously, I don't mind. I love my grill."

"No. You should enjoy yourself. Seriously, brother. It's enough that you're hosting everything."

"Don't even mention it. It makes me happy."

It did make him happy. I imagined that after the death of Terry and his injuries, he was having a hard time and wanted family around him as much as possible.

Ella and I as well as Mr. and Mrs. Carlson would stay at the mansion, with a few other brothers. Anyone else would stay in a block of hotel rooms we reserved for out of town travelers.

Compared to both Ella's and my previous wedding plans, the whole business was very low key and that was the way we both wanted it. Not that we didn't trust that the wedding would come off, but we understood what really mattered wasn't how big and expensive the wedding was, but the emotions behind it.

Those were rock-solid.

On a Monday at the end of March, while Ella and I were visiting the penthouse renovation, watching as movers brought up our furniture so we could make sure they positioned it properly in the newly finished and polished interior, I got a text message from Trent Sullivan about the case.

TRENT: Can you meet me at my office tomorrow at ten thirty? I should have the final report in my hands and want to go over it with you.

I answered quickly, eager to get it all over with. Trent had assured me that if they were going to charge me or indict Keith, they would have by now, so hopefully, they'd found evidence that exculpated Keith and MBC of any wrongdoing.

JOSH: I'll be there. What is your expectation on what the report says?

TRENT: Based on the fact they didn't arrest Keith or call for you to turn yourself in, I'd say it's just a report on why they bothered with the warrant in the first place. Hopefully, the material and old servers and equipment you provided cleared things up.

JOSH: Let's hope. See you tomorrow.

I turned to Ella who was glancing out the window at the view. "I'm going to see Trent tomorrow with the final report from the DOJ on the case. He thinks it's been dropped, and this is just a review."

Ella came to me and slipped her arms around my neck. "Oh, thank *God*," she said and leaned up to kiss me. "It's nice to get some good news on that front."

We spent the rest of the morning ensuring that the furniture was all in its proper place and that meant that the penthouse was almost move-in ready. The only thing left was to unpack all the boxes of dishes and kitchenware, plus all of our personal possessions. They were being moved on Wednesday. We would officially take possession then and would gradually clean out the old apartment.

"It'll be nice to be in here," Ella said as we stood at the huge floor to ceiling window looking out over the western edge of Central Park. I stood behind her with my arms around her, my chin resting on her head.

"It's our own place," I said. "Picked out by us, furnished by us, designed by us. It's all ours. I hope we have many happy years here."

"Me, too," she said.

I kissed the back of her neck and watched the cars driving along the streets below.

. . .

I went to meet with Trent the next day, eager to hear what the report concluded about MBC and Keith's role in any illegal financial dealings. My gut was in a knot despite the faith I had in him that he had done no wrong. He could have hired someone who was unethical and not known it. Whatever the case, I was hopeful that Trent was right, and it had been a set-up.

I arrived at the building where Trent worked and took the elevator to the boardroom where our meeting would be held. I said hello to the receptionist and after removing my coat and scarf, I went inside. There Trent was, seated at the head of the large conference table, a conference phone set up and a video screen pulled down across from him which showed an empty room. We were going to have a video conference with someone -- possibly the DOJ official in charge of the case.

"There you are," Trent said and stood up when I came over to his side. We shook hands and I took a seat beside him facing the screen. "We're just waiting for our counterparts at the DOJ to join us and go over the report."

"Good," I said and sat down, unbuttoning my suit jacket, trying to relax while we waited. Trent's admin person came into the office and bent down to me.

"Can I get you a coffee or some water?"

"Water would be nice," I said, and she nodded.

She left us for a moment and returned with a bottle of water and placed it in front of me.

When she was gone, Trent handed me a file and I opened it and saw that it was the report. It was on official DOJ letterhead and looked like a legal document. I scanned it but couldn't make out what the conclusion was based on a quick scan.

"What's the upshot?" I asked, and turned to Trent, who was busy scribbling something down in the margins of one page.

"The upshot is that MBC was set up by whoever it was who hacked you. The report doesn't identify the person who did the hack and there are some names redacted, so I assume they're people who may have forthcoming charges laid who the DOJ doesn't want us to know. James will brief us once he comes online."

"James?"

"McBride," Trent said. "My counterpart in the DOJ. He wrote the report and was in charge of the investigation."

We waited for a couple of minutes, and finally, McBride came on the line, apologizing for being late. He looked to be in his early forties, with greying hair, thinning on top and wire rimmed glasses. He looked like what I'd expect a DOJ investigator to look. Ordinary. Blend in.

"What's the upshot, James?" Trent asked, and I glanced back down to my document, turning to the last page, still unable to make out what the final conclusion was.

"We had an informant who suggested we look down a particular avenue for information that might lead to those responsible for the hack and for planting evidence," McBride said. "We were able to trace the original funding to a law office in Concord, New Hampshire."

"Concord?" I said, frowning. "What law office?"

"Apparently, a small corporate law office, Sinclair, Thompson and Monroe. We traced some of the activity to a man connected to your fiancée, Ella Carlson," McBride replied. "Derek Marshall works there as a corporate lawyer. Apparently, he hired someone off 4Chan to hack into MBC and put incriminating evidence on the servers."

"Oh, God," I said and rubbed my forehead. "That's Ella's ex-fiancé. They were going to get married and she called off the wedding when she discovered him cheating with his secretary. He lost his job working for the Governor of New Hampshire, Ella's father. It must have been an attempt to sabotage MBC to get back at her through me."

"That was our thinking as well," McBride said. On the screen, we saw McBride check his watch. "And as of right about now, he's being served with a warrant for his arrest on a number of charges relating to the hack and false report to the FBI."

I leaned back in my chair, shaking my head in amazement at the lengths some people would go to for revenge.

"Unbelievable," I said and turned to Trent. "I never even met the man, but he must have learned that I'd taken over MBC and wanted to hurt me in order to hurt Ella."

"That's what we concluded. No charges will be forthcoming against MBC or Keith Johnson. However, our techies would advise your techies to get better security protection in place. Apparently, a dozen admin personnel were targeted with a phishing attempt and one succeeded. A new staff member who maybe didn't have proper training in avoiding scams."

I nodded. "You can guarantee we won't make that mistake again. We've already hired an IT security expert to come into MBC and provide training in cyber security."

"That's good to hear," McBride said. "Well, gentlemen, unless you have other questions, I have another conference call to attend and have to say goodbye."

"Thanks," I said and nodded to McBride. "I seriously appreciate how helpful you have been through all this."

"Don't mention it."

The conference call ended, and I was left sitting with Trent, shaking my head once more at the audacity of Derek Marshall.

"Ella will be horrified when she finds out this was Derek."

"I'll bet she will be," Trent replied and gathered up his papers. "I'm just glad whoever it was tipped the Feds off about Marshall or you might be getting the warrant instead of him."

"I wonder who tipped him off? Someone in his office? Maybe the girlfriend?"

"That's for the FBI to know and us to never find out, I'm afraid. They keep their sources and methods very tightly protected."

"Of course, but I'd love to know who ratted him out. Whoever it was, I owe them a bottle of expensive Scotch."

"That you do," Trent said.

We finished up and I glanced at my watch. "Well, I better be going. I have my own meetings to attend. Thanks again for your fine work on this, Trent. I really appreciate it."

"That's why you pay me the big bucks," Trent said and reached out for a shake.

I shook Trent's hand and grabbed my coat and scarf, then took the elevator down to the lobby.

I nodded to the security guard sitting at the front desk and headed and out into the bright March morning. Outside, the cars drove by, horns blared, and pedestrians pushed past me, but I didn't care about the noise and smells of exhaust that filled the air.

Life was good.

It was really damn good. Ella and I were moving into the penthouse and in three weeks, I'd be married to the love of my life.

I arrived back at the building and went right up to my office, needing to cancel my next meeting so I could go and visit Ella and give her the news. My meeting with one of the IT people could wait. I had more important things to do.

Namely, celebrate with my fiancée.

I removed my coat and scarf and then went down the elevator to Ella's floor. I said hello to the receptionist and wound my way through the halls to her office. Her door was cracked open, and when I glanced in, I saw that she was bent over a manuscript, her brow furrowed as she read. Behind her was the huge picture window that looked out on the building beside ours. She looked totally absorbed in her work, which made me happy.

She truly loved what she was doing, even though it was a lowly unpaid position reading manuscripts we would likely never consider for publication.

I knocked on the door and opened it more, poking my head in. I felt bad about interrupting her when she was so intent on her work, but I knew she would want to know right away.

"Hey," I said, and she glanced up, blinking. When she saw me, she smiled.

"Josh," she said and pointed to the chair in front of her desk. "Come in. I was just reading."

I came in and closed the door and then went right over to her, bending down and kissing her warmly.

"Mmm," she said and rubbed my lips to wipe off her lipstick. "That was nice. I take it you had a good meeting with the DOJ?"

"I did," I said and sat down in the chair across from her.

"Well?" she said and leaned forward, her hands clasped in front of her on the desk. "Spill. What happened? Are they going to charge MBC? Keith?"

"Nope, and nope. No charges against MBC or Keith."

She let out a huge sigh. "Phew!" she said and wiped her brow dramatically. "I was hoping that would be the outcome but wasn't sure. What did the DOJ say about the hack and all the evidence of tax evasion and money laundering?"

"They said there was none and that the hack was an attempt to get MBC in trouble."

"Was it someone out to get Keith?" she asked.

"No, actually, it was someone out to get *me*." I wagged my eyebrows dramatically.

She made a face at that. "That's no good. Who would want to hurt you and why?"

I leaned forward, my hands clasped and leaning on the desk so that our faces were only a couple of feet apart.

"Derek Marshall, that's who."

Her jaw dropped open. "What?"

"Yes, Mr. Marshall hired some hacker and planted evidence, then turned in false accusations against me in order to hurt MBC. I guess he was unhappy with losing his job with your father and this was his attempt at revenge."

"Oh, my *God*," she said and sat staring off into space for a moment. "I would never have imagined he would do something like this."

"Me, either but who knows what evil lurks, right?"

"Who indeed," she said and sat quiet for a moment. "How did they learn that he did this?"

"Someone tipped the FBI off and they checked him out and voila. They found evidence that he was responsible."

"I'd like to thank whoever that was," Ella said.

"Me, too, but right now, I'd like to celebrate with my beautiful and loving fiancée. How about we go get some pastrami on rye?"

"With Matzo Ball Soup?" she asked hopefully.

I stood and held out my hand and she took it.

"With Matzo Ball Soup," I replied. "Anything for my ladylove."

23

ELLA

WE MOVED INTO THE PENTHOUSE AND SLOWLY, OVER the next week, we settled in, unpacking our personal possessions and getting the place set up for use. Both of us were busy trying to wrap up as much of our work as possible, getting the wedding plans finalized and our honeymoon plans finished so we could take the two weeks around the date off and not worry about work.

When the first week in April came around and then the second, my excitement rose as our wedding date neared. My dress arrived back from the seamstress a week before we were scheduled to fly out to LA, and I was excited to try it on and see how it fit. I went by myself to the bridal shop, and met with the seamstress, trying on the dress to make sure everything was perfect.

It was, and so she packaged it up and off I went, back to the penthouse. Josh greeted me at the door and pretended to try to see the dress, but I fought him.

"You are not going to see this until our wedding day," I said and hung the dress in the front closet. I went to the desk in my office and took a sticky note pad, writing *DO NOT PEEK* on it. Then, I placed the sticky on the garment bag to remind Josh that he was forbidden to look at it. He teased me that he was going to look before the wedding day, but I insisted he waited to see it.

"Steph thinks I look really good in it," I said to him when he came up behind me that day when I got back from the bridal shop. "That has to be good enough for you until Saturday."

"Saturday," Josh said and turned me around, pulling me into his arms. "I can't believe it's already almost here. Are you as excited as I am?"

"More," I said and kissed him.

We embraced and he squeezed my buttocks. "I'm very excited," he said and thrust his hips against mine so I could feel his erection. That sent a jolt of lust through my body and I closed my eyes.

"I'll be just as excited as you if you keep that up," I said and smiled as he kissed my throat. "Don't start anything you don't intend to finish."

"Oh, trust me. I intend to finish."

He smiled and kissed me passionately, pulling me to the bedroom, passion in his eyes.

I didn't fight.

He kissed me and I groaned when his hand reached up to squeeze my breast. He buried his face in my neck, kissing my ear, my throat and then the swell of my breast.

"I have a meeting in half an hour," he said. "So, I don't have much time."

"The way you're touching me, I won't need it," I said, my eyes closed as he pulled off my sweater dress, so I was standing in my bra and lace thong. His touch made my body swollen and ready just from the touch of his lips on my skin.

"Me, too," he murmured against my throat. He thumbed my nipple through the fabric of my lace bra, and I groaned, pressing my breast against his hand.

He squeezed my buttock greedily, and it made my core throb, because I couldn't wait for him to fill me up completely, pounding into me hard. He pulled down the fabric of my bra so that my breasts spilled out and buried his face between them, squeezing and sucking my nipples, making me squirm in need.

He removed his shirt while I unzipped his jeans, letting them fall to the ground. Beneath them, he wore boxer-briefs, and his erection was outlined clearly through the fabric.

He pushed me back onto the bed, and when I lay down, my thighs spread wide, he stood and admired me.

"You are so luscious. I'm going to lick every inch of you."

He pulled off his boxer briefs and stood naked before me, his thick erection jutting out, dripping wet. The sight of him makes my breath catch in my throat. I wanted him to fill me up with his cock, I wanted to ride him. I didn't care how. I just wanted him inside of me.

I reached down to remove my thong, but he stopped me.

"Stop," he said, his breath ragged. "Let me undress you."

He licked me over the fabric of my thong, his tongue pressing over my clit. The sensation drove me almost mad, for it was both teasing and not quite enough. Finally, he pulled them off and spread my thighs wider before licking a trail from my navel to my clit, his fingers spreading me wide.

"Oh, God," I gasped when he thrust his tongue inside of me. I shuddered and closed my eyes as he licked and sucked my clit.

"You're ready," he murmured.

"I am," I said, barely able to speak. He swirled his tongue over my entire slit, before slipping a finger inside me.

Then, he rubbed the head of his cock over my clit and it felt so good, but I wanted him inside of me.

"Fuck me now," I managed.

"You want it?" he asked, his movements on my clit agonizingly pleasurable.

"Please," I said, and he slipped inside of me, filling me up slowly. I gasped at the sensation, and when his thumb circled my clit, I knew it wouldn't take long.

It was then I realized he didn't put on a condom.

"A condom," I said, my eyes flying open.

"Crap," he said and leaned over, searching through the side table drawer. "We're out."

I glanced at him and shook my head. "We don't need one. I'm safe. I know you're safe, too."

"You sure?"

I nodded. "I've been religious taking the pill."

"Okay," he said and began thrusting and it felt so damn good without a condom. I realized that it was the very first time we'd had sex without one.

"I'm going to fuck you now," he said in a husky voice. "I'm going to make you come."

I didn't respond because I knew he would.

H ours later, after he returned from his meeting, we lay on the sofa together in front of our new gas fireplace and watched the night sky outside our huge picture windows. I thought about our first session of bareback intercourse earlier in the day.

It had been great, and I was surprised how much it excited me to think of having Josh inside of me without him wearing a condom.

"I found it incredibly sexy," I said and glanced up into his eyes.

"What? The way I moved my tongue?" he said, a gleam in his eyes. He knew exactly what I meant but was teasing me.

"No," I said and pushed his shoulder playfully. "You being inside of me with no protection."

"Ohh," he said and nodded knowingly. He leaned down and kissed me. "Whenever you want it, you can have it that way. We're getting married in a couple of weeks. We're both clean and you're on the pill, so I don't see why we can't have sex without a condom from now on."

"I agree," I said and rolled over on top of him. "In fact, like, right now."

His eyes widened but I felt his body respond beneath me and I knew that he found the prospect just as sexy as I did. We kissed and removed each other's clothes as rapidly as possible so that soon, we were both naked, only the light from the fireplace to illuminate us. It was more than enough to see him and soon he pushed me back on the sofa and knelt down between my thighs, his mouth finding me in the darkness.

That was my last conscious thought until much *much* later...

The week of our wedding arrived, and I was so excited, I had a hard time concentrating at work and sleeping at night. While I tried to read manuscripts, my mind kept returning to the wedding and the to-do list I had with everything that needed to be done. I had it tucked beside my desk calendar, and periodically, I pulled it out and looked it over, noting what I had left to do and what I had already done. Luckily, Steph had taken care of her side of things and had picked out a dress that she was happy to wear. I glanced at it in the catalog and then at the picture of her wearing it and was pleased. She looked wonderful.

I had my luggage open on my dresser and had been adding to it each day, planning what I'd need for the stay in LA at David's mansion and then at the all-inclusive resort where we were staying in Bora Bora. I kept the brochure open on the suitcase so I could look at it and imagine our week of peace and quiet in the luxurious house we'd rented right on the water.

I finished up all my work on Tuesday, and it was a good thing, because I had Wednesday off, so Josh and I could finalize all our plans. We were leaving for LA on Thursday, and would arrive late that afternoon, driving to David's mansion and spending Friday getting last-minute preparations for the wedding and dinner ready. My parents and Steph were flying together and would arrive in LA late on Thursday night. All of us would spend Friday together, and then have the wedding party dinner that night with the brothers. The wedding was Saturday.

We stayed in LA overnight and then would fly to Bora Bora on Sunday, arriving back the following Saturday night. We had that Sunday off and then it was back to work on Monday morning for us both.

My mother might have dreamed of a big wedding with hundreds of relatives, but after Josh and my previous experiences, a small wedding was pretty much all we could consider. There would be no announcement in any paper, and no big venue, no bridal shower, no gift registry.

All in all, it would be a very casual, very intimate wedding and short honeymoon, but that was the way Josh and I both wanted it.

. . .

Thursday arrived and I barely slept, waking up several times, my mind going over what was left to do, but everything seemed well under control. All we had to do now was finish packing, grab our tickets and passports, and head to the airport.

We'd arrive at LAX, get a rental car, and drive to David's place in the hills. Unpack, and then greet my parents and Steph, spend some time together with the Macintyre brothers getting to know one another. Friday, we'd pick up the last-minute items we needed for the wedding – ribbons, flowers, folding chairs, small gifts for the wedding party. We'd go over the menu for the wedding party dinner, which David insisted on grilling. Then, we'd confirm everything with the caterer for our wedding dinner.

We had our tickets for Bora Bora and our second suitcases packed for it.

Sunscreen, a tiny bikini, and not much else.

I touched everything, ticking it off the list I had in my hand with a big red checkmark to note it had been done and was ready.

Then I turned to Josh.

"I'm all set. How about you?"

He shrugged and counted the suitcases. "Ready." Then he came over to me and slipped his arms around my waist, pulling me against his body. "Are you excited, my almost-future wife and love of my life?"

"I am, my almost-future husband and love of my life."

"Then, let's go."

We did.

Josh and I carried the suitcases down to the lobby, where a limo was waiting for us to take us to JFK. The limo driver helped with the luggage while I climbed into the back seat and waited for Josh to join me. He finally slid in beside me and we fastened our seat belts.

Josh took hold of my hand and kissed my knuckles.

"Seven months," he said.

"I know," I replied and smiled. "Only seven months. It's hard to believe that it all started just out there, a few feet away."

"I'm am so glad you're a jaywalker."

He leaned in to kiss me warmly and I closed my eyes, my happiness overflowing, making my eyes tear up.

"Me, too."

Then we were off, driving through Manhattan towards the airport and the rest of our lives.

24

JOSH

Our flight to L.A. was uneventful, and our plane arrived late in the afternoon. After waiting for our bags, we rented a vehicle and drove the rest of the way to David's place in Brentwood.

When we arrived, the brothers gathered in the entry, and we all hugged and slapped each other on the back. We spent some time with David and the other brothers while we waited for Ella's parents and Steph to arrive later that night. In the interim, we enjoyed a barbecue around the pool, with David as host, cooking our steaks and grilling lobster tails and corn on the cob.

When Steph and Ella's parents finally arrived, Ella and I went to greet them. We had a round of hugs and kisses as we greeted each other. Steph was suitably impressed by David's place. Even for someone who was growing used to the idea of my family's wealth, it was pretty overwhelming. She stood in the entry and glanced around, noticing the marble and waterfall.

David entered the house from the patio where he had been swimming and came right over, shaking Ella's father's hand and giving her mom a hug. He looked every inch the debauched rocker, wearing nothing but a pair of black swim trunks and sandals, his very buff body on display with its tatted arms and chest as he toweled off. He wore gold earrings in his ears, his hair was longish and dark brown, his beard was well-trimmed, and he had a brilliant smile. I could easily understand why female fans were so enamored with him.

I'd heard women describe him as gorgeous.

I introduced Steph, and when he saw her, David wolf-whistled.

"So, *you're* the best friend Ella told me about," David said, giving Steph a hug. "I hope you realize that we're partners in crime at the wedding, since I'm going to be Josh's best man."

"The David *Macintyre*," she said and shook her head. "I can't believe I'm meeting you. I've been a fan for years. Can I get a selfie for my Facebook page? My friends back in Concord won't believe it without photographic evidence."

David seemed especially pleased and gave her a big smile. "Always glad to meet a fan and take a picture with them."

They stood close together and Steph took out her cell, snapping a photo of the two of them together.

"Thanks so much," she said and turned in a circle. "This house screams super-rich rock star. I'm suitably impressed."

"I know," he said and glanced around with her. "I can't claim any credit since I didn't pick it. My investment advisor did. I didn't decorate it. My interior designer did so none of this is me. The only things I can claim are the waterfall and the infinity pool. They're mine."

"Infinity pool?" Steph said with a squeal of delight. "Oh, my God, I can't wait to try it out."

"Put on your swimsuit and give it a try. Michael and Christian are already in it. It's warm, too. It gets cool at night in April, so I have the heat lamps on."

"You call this cool?" Steph said with a laugh. "You should be in Manhattan this time of year."

"No, thanks," David said. "I'll take LA. I find it cold today."

Ella took Steph upstairs to her bedroom and to help her get unpacked. I turned to her parents and grabbed two of their suitcases, hauling them upstairs to their room, which was in the same wing as Steph's bedroom. I left them to unpack and then headed downstairs to the patio, where my brothers were assembled.

"There he is," Nash said and gave me a thump on the back. "The groom, enjoying his last hours of freedom."

"You mean my last hours of living the lonely bachelor's existence?" I countered. "How soon before the rest of you find your bliss?"

"I already found mine," David said. "Music's my mistress."

"Flight is mine," Nash replied, his arms crossed.

"I'm still taking care of business," Michael replied. "Too busy for romance."

"No one's too busy for romance," I replied.

We all turned to Christian, who was in the pool, his arms on the side while he watched us.

"Don't look at me," he said. "I'm too busy teaching and planning to become leader of the free world to fall in love."

"Such diminished lives you guys lead," I said with a scoff. "Rock star. Presidential-wanna-be. Bush pilot. Builder. None of you know what you're missing. I recommend finding yourself a beautiful loving woman as your partner. You'll be a lot happier if you do, no matter what you think you're too busy doing."

"I'm happy as a lark being single," David said. "I have too many women, in fact. Don't know how I could choose only one."

"Ha! Said like a man who's lonely in a crowd. We were meant to form pair bonds, brother," I said and slapped David on the back. "We're only really happy when we have that one special love. Seriously. Try it some time."

"Sure, sure," he said and slapped me on the back. "Whatever you say, brother. For right now, I'm happy with the way things are. There are a million beautiful women in this city ripe for the picking and all I have to do is pick one after the other after the other. The world is my oyster." He held his arms out and turned in a circle, gesturing to LA, which was spread out below us, the lights of the city like a million gems in the darkness.

"That it is," I said with a laugh and gave him a hug. "I found the pearl. You can keep looking."

"You did," David said and squeezed my shoulder. "You really did find your pearl. Ella is a sweet *sweet* woman and you're a lucky man, I gotta say I know how happy you are with her."

"This too could be yours, if only you'd let yourself fall in love," I said.

"I fall in love all the time," he replied. "None of them have been the one, I guess. Maybe one day."

"One day, you'll fall hard. I'll enjoy watching."

Ella and Steph arrived, and both were in their bathing suits, large beach towels wrapped around themselves. Steph was very tall, and attractive, with lean curves and an attractive physique. I saw Christian eyeing her while she and Ella removed their towels and climbed down into the warm infinity pool. All my brothers enjoyed the show, and I wondered if anyone would hit on Steph while she was in L.A.

Mr. and Mrs. Carlson came down and joined us, and the nine of us sat around the pool and talked about the wedding and Ella and my honeymoon in Bora Bora.

Finally, when it was getting close to midnight, David stood up and cleared his throat.

"I'm hitting the hay, but if you want to stay up later, by all means, please feel free. Just make sure to lock the patio doors when you come in. We have a fun day tomorrow, and the only thing any of us have to do is memorize where we'll stand during the ceremony and what, if any words we have to say during the ceremony or after at the dinner. See you in the morning. I have Estelle coming to make us a nice brunch so you can expect the full deal at around nine. For those of you who get up early, you'll have to wait. The early bird will not get the worm, in this case."

We all said goodnight and made our way upstairs to our respective rooms. Before we went up, Mr. Carlson stopped me at the bottom of the staircase.

"Come join me in the kitchen for a minute," he said quietly. He turned to Mrs. Carlson. "We'll be up in a minute. Go on ahead."

I walked with him to the kitchen, figuring he wanted to ask me about the FBI case. We didn't get a chance to talk privately about it since I got the news.

"What's up, Governor?" I asked, still not feeling able to call him 'Dad' or 'Father'.

"Please, call me Emmet." He took a glass out of the cupboard and filled it with ice and water from the refrigerator dispenser. Then he turned to me.

"I wanted to ask you about the case. I heard that MBC was hacked and that some fake evidence was planted to make one of your execs guilty of tax evasion."

"And money laundering," I added, nodding.

He nodded. "I wanted you to know that when I heard, I suggested that the FBI check out Derek."

"It was you who tipped them off?" I asked, shocked that it had been Ella's father. "What made you think of it?"

"He threatened me," Emmet said quietly, glancing around like he was concerned who would overhear him. "I didn't tell Ella or her mother. I didn't want to worry them, but he wanted to hurt me, and he wanted to hurt Ella because of losing his position and the hit he took to his reputation. When I heard that MBC had been hacked, I called a contact I have in the FBI and suggested they check out Derek. I had a hunch. It was right."

"Wow," I said, shaking my head in surprise. "I had no idea it was you who tipped them off. Thank you. I trusted my CFO to not have done what the FBI alleged, and I expected he would be cleared, but still. It was pretty touch and go for a while."

"I'm sure it was," he said and cleared his throat like talking about it was difficult for him. "You have to understand that at one time, I thought Derek would be my son-in-law. I truly loved him as a son for a while, but he was more ambitious than he was ethical. Unfortunately, power attracts the worst as well as the best."

"That it does," I said. Then I decided to be totally honest with him. "I want you to know that I had nothing to do with MBC's investigation into your partner's activities back in the day. I was still in college--."

He held up his hand and stopped me. "Don't mention it. We'll put all that behind us and have a détente, okay?"

"Sounds good to me," I said and then I frowned, remembering how suspicious I was about Emmet getting off without any charges, considering it was his business partner who was found guilty of so much.

"So, you had no idea that Garner was involved in anything shady back in the day?" I asked, pouring myself a glass of ice water.

"Actually," he said and leaned against the countertop. "It was me who turned him in."

He raised his eyebrows meaningfully. I mulled that over for a moment.

"You suspected him of cheating and tipped off the Feds?"

"I was working for them," he said softly, taking a sip of water, considering me through narrowed eyes. "And that has to stay completely between you and me. Neither Ella or her mother know."

"You were working for the *Feds*?" My mouth dropped open in total shock.

"I did a stint in Military Intelligence when I was with the Army before I went to law school. When I got out, I helped out with some fraud and money laundering cases as an informant."

"Wow," I said and was truly nonplussed by the news. Emmet had worked for the DOJ providing them with intelligence he'd gleaned through his contacts in the business world. "That puts a whole different spin on things."

"It does. I can't let on to people that I'm a friend of the DOJ or they'd clam up, but I do my part to bring the guilty to justice. Just so you know your father-in-law isn't a crook." I glanced at him to gauge his mind set but he was hard to read. Finally, he gave me a grin.

"That's good to know," I said with a relieved laugh. We shook hands.

"Welcome to the family, Son," he said and gave me a quick hug.

"Thanks, Dad."

I said it and it didn't feel so strange. I was glad that I knew the truth about him now – how he'd offered up his once-upon-a-time future son-in-law as a suspect in the hacking case against MBC, and how he'd been working for the Feds all along.

"Don't say anything to Ella, but if you do, and I'm sure you will because young couples these days tend to tell everything to each other, tell her it is imperative that she never *ever* says a word about it to anyone. Not Steph. Not her mother. My life could depend on it. If my enemies knew, I'd be dead."

"Mum's the word, and Emmet?" I said and gripped his arm. "Thanks for telling me and for what you did for MBC."

He shook his head. "It was for Ella. You love her and be good to her and make me happy that I did."

"I do and I will."

With that, we each went up to our respective bedrooms in David's mansion in the Hollywood Hills.

That night, I lay in bed and debated whether to tell Ella what Emmet told me. He didn't want me to tell her, for her own sake, but he also knew I probably would. I knew he'd served in the military, but I didn't know he'd been in military intelligence. His bio said he'd been in planning, so I had no idea exactly what he did while he served.

"Can't sleep?" Ella asked when I tossed and turned.

S. E. LUND

"Big day tomorrow," I said and pulled her against me. "Lots on my mind."

"No cold feet, I hope," she said softly.

I rubbed my feet against hers. "Nope. Hot as usual."

I kissed her and felt her smile against my lips.

It was then that I decided to tell Ella what Emmet had told me, because of my pledge to always tell her everything. We would soon be married, and I felt so damn good knowing that my fears about Emmet were misplaced and he was in fact a very good man with strong ethics and morals.

He was a man I could respect. A man much like my father, in his own way.

Hopefully, one day, a man I could love like a father.

So, I told her.

"Oh, my God, Josh..." She sat up and turned on the bedside light, and then leaned over me, her hands on either side of my shoulders. "My father was working with the Justice Department to rat on his partner?"

"He was an informant and was helping them fight financial fraud. He suspected Derek when he learned MBC had been hacked because he was being personally threatened and figured it was Derek."

We talked for a while and I tried to assuage her fears for her father and mother.

"I hope Derek goes away to jail for this," Ella said.

"I have no doubt that he will. Hopefully for long enough that he's suitably chastised by the time he comes out."

She turned off the light and lay back down beside me. I pulled her into my arms, and we snuggled down together.

"I'm glad the two of you are now going to be on better terms," she said softly.

"Me, too," I said and sighed. "For a while, I was suspicious about your father and why he didn't get charged when his partner did, but now I understand. He was working with the Feds to bring his partner down."

"He always seemed so angry about it," Ella said.

"He was probably putting on a show, so he'd be in good with the bad guys. Keep his cover."

"I guess so," Ella said and yawned.

"You're not supposed to tell anyone about it. Technically, neither of us are supposed to know and your father asked me not to tell you. Whatever you do, don't let on to your mother. She doesn't know."

"I won't," Ella said and leaned up to kiss me. "Thank you for telling me."

"I said I'd tell you everything and I meant it."

"I did, too," she replied and snuggled back down and together, we both tried to fall asleep.

The day of our wedding dawned clear and warm – perfect for an outdoor ceremony late in the afternoon. Steph and Ella spent the morning at a spa getting their bodies waxed, moisturized, massaged, manicured, pedicured and their hair washed and styled. David and I did our own masculine version of a grooming spa and Ella and I ate separately, trying our best to avoid seeing each other on the day of the wedding. Ella slept in Steph's room so we could start the day right and so when the time came for us to get dressed and for Ella to walk down the makeshift aisle between two rows of folding chairs to where I waited with David at my side, my emotions were high.

When I saw her, I felt my heart swell with happiness.

She was *beautiful*.

Her hair was up and there were wild flowers in her bouquet and in her hair. The dress was simple but beautiful, matching her own pure beauty.

I felt a choke in my throat as the ceremony proceeded. It was simple, just the way Ella and I wanted. The officiant was a female pastor in the Presbyterian Church that was in the Brentwood neighborhood whom David enlisted to do the ceremony. Before we left for LA, we'd written out our vows, and they pretty much mirrored what we had said to each other weeks earlier.

We stood facing each other and when the time came, we repeated them to each other:

Don't ever doubt my feelings for you. If you need me to, I will happily tell you that I love you every day of my life for the rest of my life.

When I slipped the ring onto her finger and kissed her, I knew we both meant it.

We turned and faced the small group of our family and a few friends, husband and wife and I thought about what my father had written in his will:

My one piece of advice on how to have a happy life? Marry well. Have a family with many children. Love your family with all your heart, the way I did you and your mother.

I knew with a certainty that went right to my heart and soul that he was right.

EPILOGUE

Ella

AFTER A WONDERFUL WEEK IN BORA BORA, JOSH AND I arrived back in Manhattan, tanned and rested, ready for our new life together. Both of us went right back to work the day after we arrived home and it felt good to be back in my office with a pile of manuscripts in front of me, waiting to be read. We put our heads down and focused on work for the first month back, and it wasn't unusual for us both to be working late in the office until eight or nine at night, breaking only to have dinner together in one of our respective offices.

Towards the end of the first month back at work, I felt unwell, and decided to go back to the penthouse early. It was early June and the weather was unseasonably warm. I figured I had just overheated on the way back from my walk through Central Park for exercise.

Before I left the office, I checked my calendar to see what stage of my cycle I was in and noticed that I was late for my period.

I frowned and double-checked, but sure enough, I was a week late. I must have gotten out of sync due to the wedding and honeymoon, but that was to be expected. Sometimes, when a woman went through a particularly exciting or stressful period in her life, hormones would be out of whack. When Jerkface and I split, my cycle was all messed up, despite taking the pill.

I stopped at the pharmacy on my way home and picked up a pregnancy test just in case. I doubted I was pregnant, because I had taken the pill religiously for years, but we had been having sex without a condom for months.

Nothing was out of the realm of possibility...

Josh arrived home at the usual time and plopped down beside me on the sofa.

"Are you feeling better?" he asked and leaned over to kiss me.

"Yes," I said and smiled. "I had a cup of peppermint tea and it settled my stomach."

"That's good. Was it something you ate for lunch? Leftovers?"

I shook my head and reached into the pocket of my robe.

"It's this."

I handed him the pregnancy test, which was positive.

He stared at it, and his jaw fell open. Then he turned to me and the expression in his eyes told me everything I needed to know.

He was ecstatic.

"Oh, Ellie," he said and pulled me onto his lap, his face buried in my neck. "I'm so happy." He kissed me tenderly. "Are you happy?"

He looked at me, his blue eyes searching mine out.

"I couldn't be happier."

"What about your MA at Columbia?"

I shrugged. "I can do it whenever I want. Columbia isn't going anywhere."

"You're sure? We can hire nannies and babysitters and you'll have all the support you need if you want to go."

"I'm fine. I'm happy, Josh. We love each other. We want a family. We're going to have a family."

I smiled, tears of happiness in my eyes.

He kissed me and I knew that whatever happened, we would face it together.

THE END

ABOUT THE AUTHOR

S. E. Lund writes erotic, contemporary, new adult and paranormal romance. She lives with her family of humans and animals in Beautiful British Columbia Canada on the side of a mountain and in sight of an active volcano. She dreams of living in a warm climate where snow is just a word in a dictionary.

For More Information:
www.selundauthor.com
selund2012@gmail.com

Sign up for S. E. Lund's newsletter — she hates spam and will never share your info:

http://eepurl.com/1Wcz5

ALSO BY S. E. LUND

THE UNRESTRAINED SERIES:

THE AGREEMENT: Book 1 in the Unrestrained Series

THE COMMITMENT: Book 2 in the Unrestrained Series

UNRESTRAINED: Book 3 in the Unrestrained Series

UNBREAKABLE: Book 4 in the Unrestrained Series

FOREVER AFTER: Book 5 in the Unrestrained Series

EVERLASTING: Book 6 in the Unrestrained Series

DRAKE FOREVER: Book 7 in the Unrestrained Series

ENDLESS: Book 8 in the Unrestrained Series

THE UNRESTRAINED SERIES COLLECTION ONE
(BOOKS 1 - 3)

THE UNRESTRAINED SERIES COLLECTION ONE
(BOOKS 4 - 6)

THE DRAKE SERIES:

DRAKE RESTRAINED: Book 1 in the Drake Series

DRAKE UNWOUND: Book 2 in the Drake Series

DRAKE UNBOUND: Book 3 in the Drake Series

THE MACINTYRE BROTHERS SERIES

Tempt Me: Book One

Tease Me: Book Two

Tame Me: Book Three

STANDALONE BOOKS:

MR. BIG SHOT

MATCHED

IF YOU FALL

THE BAD BOY SERIES:

BAD BOY SAINT: Book 1 in the Bad Boy Series

BAD BOY SINNER: Book 2 in the Bad Boy Series

BAD BOY SOLDIER: Book 3 in the Bad Boy Series

BAD BOY SAVIOR: Book 4 in the Bad Boy Series

THE BAD BOY SERIES COLLECTION: All 4 books together in one volume.

PARANORMAL ROMANCE SERIES:

DOMINION: BOOK 1

ASCENSION: BOOK 2

RETRIBUTION: BOOK 3

RESURRECTION: BOOK 4

REDEMPTION: BOOK 5

THE DOMINION SERIES COMPLETE COLLECTION